BloodMinazue

GUILLERMO F. PORRO III

©2017

BloodMinazue

For information about this title or to order other books and/or
electronic media, contact:

Guillermo Porro

dadeshark19@yahoo.com

ISBN: 978-0-692-17179-0 Paperback

Printed in the United States of America
Cover and Interior Design: Infinity Flower Publishing, LLC

In memory of Brian Meizlik.

Thank you to him, my father, and all of my friends whom I have had the honor to enjoy adventures with as I searched for growth and rewards.

Table of Contents

Table of Contents

Prologue

Within the northern continent, the land remains a bundle of terrain diversity. From chains of volcanic mountains to lush forests that make up most of the open lands. Meanwhile in the center of a hilly field, Dapalos the Minazue capital allows just about everyone inside the city walls without harm, the guards wear heavily durable armor and carry weapons the size of a steer's head at their sides as they keep watch. They are ever alert for disturbances, not only from disruptive members of their own clan, but from the dastardly rival clan that stands just a mere body of water away, the Barazul.

A group of races that came together to fight off the bloody invaders trying to take control of their land, the Minazue have not always been the most tranquil. At the head of this clan is the group known as the Minazue syndicate. They are the elite of the elite, who station themselves just out of reach of the commoners, inside Dapalos's sister city, Maznaro. The syndicate consists of a single member from each race, sitting side by side, discussing battle preparations, leadership duties, and ways to grow their civilization. Previously, the common folk would have never seen such a scene of unity. The idea of the Gorioc Elves and the Vorae orcs from the volcanic lands going from rivals to teammates seemed suicidal, yet they grew stronger with a united front, even taking in other leaders from the smaller clans such as the Hazel people who control the animals and trees throughout the land and the misfits from beyond the grave who return either as undead or flesh-melting zombies. Reasons for such unification can be broad from a need of peace to keeping your allies closer than approaching enemies. In this case, a great war for natural resources sent a crack down the center of the world, separating two continents by a large body of water. Dragons flew out from the clouds, breathing fire even as the sky rained arrows onto both sides. War waged from the tree tops of every forest to the deepest depths of the sea. The Barazul led by their current king, charged their way with demands of taking the arcane veins in the ground from themselves. However, the Minazue stood in their way and the way of their demonic creations.

Many lost their lives throughout the great war, and even those that survived had to rebuild their lives as the land remained fractured. Life was almost suffocated into extinction when magic came into the picture, along with items containing mythical properties, which shifted the idea of waging a battle. Sorcerers began to bring forth psychotic, inhuman creatures, such as Mana breakers or those meant to eviscerate the life and will-power out of their opposition. Other monsters began to appear as well, such as massive creatures that can soar with the mountains while hiding behind portals to keep their identities secret, as well as magical creatures that rise from the very elements that make up our world. Forced to shift their strategy, the Minazue sent a team of fighters into the mountains where they forged weapons inside the darkest caves which contained the most powerful streams of magic. They shifted the odds as it sent the Barazul retreating onto their boats as they disappeared into the horizon. With their enemies fading in the distance, the creatures retreated into myths and legends. As the smoke spun softly into the sky, the magic within the weapons faded causing them to turn to ash. With no weapons, the Minazue remained on defense for years, waiting for the Barazuls armies return. However even as the armies retreated, small troops remained behind hidden by magic to protect them from being persecuted.

Lately, additions to the syndicate have been sparse, as peace came swiftly with the addition of these groups. This brings us to this very day into a setting where two tribes remain on edge as they wait for another reason for war. Yet even as motive grows thin, new missions appear causing their attentions to shift. Dragons the size of skyscrapers and mobs of united creatures spread throughout, holding keys to great treasure. This brings us through the open gate of Maznaro and those that live within, trying to find their designated quest of riches.

Chapter One

A crack of lightning sets the scene, light reflecting off the various building around the city, bones making up the structures while various races interact along the paths throughout. In this city known as Maznaro, there is only one place that can tolerate such chaos at this time. That place, Xelavern, is a tavern like many others in the city. Grog and beer is guzzled down by the glass as the orcs mix with the non-living to tell tales long and old inside a two-story room filled to the brim with occupants. They either surround circular tables or jostle in front of a counter, where an animal-shifting barkeeper provides the drinks. The raucous atmosphere falls just short of violent as the creatures and beings of all kinds test out their armors, from the shiny new metals fresh from the mines to lighter, leather skins which give a chance to those with lesser upper body strength.

Weapons of all shapes and sizes lean against the front wall, from swords to maces, and even axes fresh from the day's battle. Blood dripping from the weapons drops down into a grate which absorbs it, preventing any excuse for an accident. See, this room isn't just filled with average civilians, there are also the barbaric, the explosive, and some of the most holy fighters in the land, all coming together in a single room for boisterous socializing. However, not all are amid the fray; some prefer the dark crevices in the room. Hiding in the shadows, thieves and rogues sit amongst one another, comparing their hauls of coins and gems inside their pouches.

Inside Xelavern, the occupants drop to a hush when suddenly

the front door crashes along the floor, splintering at the foot of the bar counter. A shadow makes its way along the ground and slithers between the tables. As everyone watches in silence, the shadow stops just shy of the door and starts to bubble. From within the depths of the darkness, a large half-breed male pops out and stands on top of the puddle. Wearing a dark robe which covers most of his skin, the man drops his hood, revealing a skull mask around his head. He reaches inside his robe, causing some to manifest their wands in protection. The man pauses as he watches the various twinkles of light around the room.

"Pardon me, but I hear you can get a good grog here," he says, pulling his hand back out from his robe.

"We don't serve your kind here," the bartender replies, handing a drink over to the one of the sorcerers next to the bar.

"What kind would that be?" the man asks, raising his other hand, a purplish flame wrapping around it. Once more the room twinkles with magic, when suddenly the flame sinks back into his hand, turning into a human skull.

"Sybolisk," the bartender replies, sending a hush throughout the room.

The man smirks, showing off his bright white canines, which protrude over his bottom lip. He turns the skull's face towards him before turning his attention back to the bartender. "I mean no harm, just a simple drink before heading off on my Gaizall."

"Do you even have any coin?" the bartender asks. The others around the counter look over at the man as he makes his way over to one of the tables nearby.

He stops and places the skull down onto the table as two armor-wielding fellows push themselves back. He turns back to the bartender and reaches inside his robe, suddenly struggling to get his hand back out. After a couple of moments, the man yanks his hand free, revealing the carcass of a creature whose skin was as blue as the sky above. Its scaly skin falling off, the carcass's amphibious features cause the man to struggle to keep it upright. "How did that get in there?"

"Do you have coin or not?" the bartender asks once more, this time with a touch of anger.

The man drops the creature on the floor, allowing its blue blood to leach out as he reaches inside his robe once more. This time, he pulls out a black bag with silver lacing at the top which he opens to the awaiting bartender. He flips it over, a mound of gold coins piling on the table. "I believe this should be enough."

"Fine Sybolisk, take a seat here in front," the barkeeper replies, turning his back to the man.

"The name is Prozper," the man replies, making his way over to the open bar seat in from of him.

On both sides of him, bulky warriors wrap their hands around their own glasses, watching him suspiciously. Looking down, Prozper takes in the warped red fabric that covers the barstool before looking up at the bartender. He takes a seat, lifting one of his hands over his shoulder. The skull on the table starts to vibrate before suddenly launching toward Prozper's hand. Once inside his grasp, Prozper places the skull down onto the wooden counter as he looks up at the bartender.

The bartender turns around with a brown flask as he looks down at Prozper's skeletal glass. Without a word, the bartender tilts the flask, causing the grog within to fill up the skull. Just before it can overflow, the bartender lifts the flask back up, causing the beer to stop flowing. As he places the container down on the shelf beneath the counter, the bartender tilts his head toward the face of the skull. "How does it not leak out?"

"What do you mean?" Prozper asks, following his gaze.

The bartender lifts his wrinkly fingers and points over to the eye sockets.

"Magic," Prozper says tauntingly.

The bartender rolls his eyes as he steps away.

Smiling, Prozper wraps his hand around the skull. His gray skin camouflaging the bone, he lifts it toward his mouth. He reveals his sharp teeth momentarily before placing the skull between them. Gulping loudly, Prozper chugs down the grog before slamming the skull onto the counter and wiping his mouth with the sleeve of his robe. Taking a satisfied breath, Prozper looks back over at the bartender, seeing him at the other end of the counter serving another guest. He starts to order more as a dull murmur fills the room again, when a sudden groan catches his ears.

Prozper spins on his chair, seeing another shadow creeping through the doorway. The groan fills the room, the occupants turning to watch as the dead creature's body reanimates. Prozper watches as the newly-animated corpse crawls its way toward the door, leaving behind it a trail of blood as it passes by the final set of tables. Prozper turns back to the counter before lifting his hand, snapping his fingers. The sound echoes through the room as, beneath him, a puddle of darkness bubbles and slides its way across the floor, sucking up the blood as it goes, returning the flooring to normal. The puddles streaks toward the wounded creature as it struggles to escape.

The creature wraps its claws around the door frame just as the pool of darkness appears underneath it. With a sucking sound, the puddle opens up, the creature screaming as it falls into the shadow, which itself disappears into the floor. Prozper glances over and smirks at a job well done before turning back to the counter. He draws a surprised breath when he realizes the seats around him are now empty, even as the rest of the room bubbles with action.

Shrugging to himself, Prozper turns his attention to the wall in front of him, seeing various mementos hanging about, mostly cheap and useless pieces of treasure, except for the ones at the very top. To the left hung a torn piece of black cloth with a red symbol fading on top of it, while on the right a single flag representing the opposition to the Minazue.

"BARTENDER!"

The bartender turns around and faces Prozper, whose crystal blue eyes are focused on the wall. "What's wrong with you, Sybolisk? Can only handle one drink?"

The rest of the bar lets out a chuckle as Prozper's grayish skin begins to redden as he turns his eyes on the bartender. "No, however, you appear to be a Barazul lover."

The bar quiets as the bartender makes his way over to Prozper before stopping in front of him. With a snarl, he looks over his shoulder at the two objects that caught Prozper's attention. "That flag you see be from the chest of King Ronos, the fallen Barazul leader."

"And the other?" Prozper asks. He watches as the bartender's skin shifts from a bark-like material to pastey white as he looks at the wall.

"That is the crest of the BloodMinazue."

Prozper spins on his chair, a humanoid being with pale green skin stepping into the reddish lighting. He moves toward the counter, pulling off his hat to reveal his orcish features, which surprises Prozper as he sits next to him. His teeth jut from either side of his mouth as he turns to reveal mismatching eyes, one icy blue and the other pitch black.

"Who are you?" the bartender demands.

"The name is Groza and I am a proprietor of all that is Blood-Minazue," Groza replies, placing a large bag down onto the counter.

To their surprise, its weight causes the counter to bend, and they watch as Groza places his hands within the opening and spreads it wider. Once it was large enough, Groza reaches inside, struggling to pull something out of it. Finally, after a couple of muscle-straining moments the bag re-shapes as a giant book appears in his hands. He places it down on the counter in between the empty mugs, causing the others to look over. His uncut nails skim the sides of the book as he pulls at the top cover.

"How long ago were they around?" Prozper asks.

"They are still around, however, without this epic adventure we might not still be enjoying our territory," Groza replies.

"So how did you come into possession of this book? And what even is it?" Prozper asks. Looking down at the black silken material, Prozper notices a similar reddish logo covering much of the cover.

"I personally transcribed this on my journey to learn more about their quest," Groza replies. He watches as Prozper reaches for the book before pulling it closer to him.

Prozper flips open the cover, revealing brownish pages and lines of writing that fill the pages. He flips the pages carefully, his eyes darting across the words. He suddenly slams the cover, nearly bending the pages as he turns back to Groza. "How did you get the Barazul side of things?"

"From the prisoners within the dungeon underneath Dapalos," Groza replies, taking back possession of the book.

"Well, I don't know about my nature-loving friend here, but I'm curious to hear this story," Prozper says, turning his attention to the bartender.

"I am too. Also, I think that nasty druid gave me a rancid potion," the bartender replies.

Before either of them can reply, the bartender's eyes turn pitch black and his face starts to morph. Spherical features take over his mouth and nose, his nostril enlarging as his skin whitens despite the lighting in the room. A thin layer of fur grows along his skin as a black circle forms around one of his eyes. More circles form on each arm as his fingers melt away and turn into hooves. The bartender staggers back as two horns curve from behind his ears. Once the horns were in place, he reaches his hand back, feeling the points against his hooves. Disoriented, he shakes his head as he steps back up to the counter.

"Are you feeling okay?" Prozper asks as Groza places his hand along the edge of the cover.

"Either it's the alcohol, or you just grew a tail!" one of the elves slurs from down the counter.

The bartender struggles to turn around, his eyes catching sight of a long tail sticking from out his backside, ending in a plume of black hair. His eyes wide with shock, the bartender spins his head around, looking over at Groza. "Get a moooove on and start reading it," he snaps. "This should wear off with time."

Groza nods his head, struggling to hide a smirk as he looks down at the book, flipping to the first page of writing. As he clears his throat, the remaining noises around the room fade away into silence, allowing him to have the floor. "Let the story begin with how the first major battle between the Barazul and Minazue starts."

Chapter Two

The journey starts in the center of a section of land surrounded by a mixture of grass and trees. A campsite spans the hillside with leather tents and stone buildings spread throughout. Giant barriers of stone encircle the camp, where the strongest guards stand watch. Their attire was unlike any seen in the major cities, only robes made of the lightest metals in the land. Gems surround them, providing power to the guards as they keep their hands steady above their wands. This campsite was unlike any other, built for the practitioners of the arcane and the magic brought forth by nature. Beyond the wooden logs that make up the front gate, the residents proceed with various activities to maintain their arcane wisdom, from juggling fireballs shot out by their apprentices, to spinning objects as they levitate just above the palms of their hand.

Just beyond the center of camp, within the main building, wind spins around a room, a bluish dome sitting in the center. Within its heart, a being levitates with his legs beneath him. His stoic features, hidden behind radical bands of brown hair, struggle to contain themselves against the force of his aura. The being, known as Crimpste, is the leader of the mages.

As he sits in a trance above the floor, glowing scrolls extend themselves along the ground. Their writing glows brightly as Crimpste's eyes fly open, shattering the dome and calming the wind. He touches his feet on the cold ground as the end of his robe settles just shy of his ankles. He quickly finds a pair of cloth sandals and slips them on before turning toward the door. Suddenly, one of the scrolls glows brighter than the rest, manifesting a fireball. Snapping away from the scroll, the fireball erupts and strikes the door, shattering it as Crimpste looks on. He sprints out the doorway, his eyes searching along the towers to find two guards extending their heads over the railing.

"Master, is everything okay?" Apocol asks from behind him.

"Apocol, have you seen anything out of the ordinary?" Crimpste replies, making his way over to a circular staircase.

"Well, besides you blowing up your door, I can't say I have," Apocol answers, looking over at Shlippmack shaking his head.

"This is no time to be funny, just answer the question," Crimpste yells shortly before arriving at the top of the wall. He then walks over to Apocol, occasionally glancing over to the horizon.

Apocol turns his head to look over at the same area before returning his attention to Crimpste. "I don't see any danger outside these walls and haven't for a while."

"Just trees and the occasional migration of animals making their way back and forth," Shlippmack adds.

"That is thanks to the power of Shlippmack and Crusayder," Apocol says, lowering his cowl to reveal his elven ears. As his black hair flow beneath his robe, he turns to Shlippmack.

"All for the safety of all mages," Shlippmack mumbles as he bows with his face toward the gray floor.

"Your deed has not gone unnoticed Shlippmack," Crimpste replies.

Shlippmack lifts his head up to see Apocol motioning to him as he looks over at Crimpste still looking out into the horizon.

Crimpste continues to look around the camp, stopping suddenly when he notices a disturbance far off down the stone road. "What's that?"

He points in the direction of an opening between the lines of trees, causing the others to turn toward it. Blinking against the sunlight, they step forward to try to get a better look. As all three lean against the railing, Crimpste steps back from the railing and turns around, catching sight of a small group of mages within the courtyard below.

"Canosan, stop your teachings and come up here," he calls to them. He then watches as the man pauses before quickly climbing the stairs.

"Yes, Master Crimpste, how can I be of service?" Canosan asks, his students behind him.

"I want you to bring Scurge and that scroll of his to me immediately," commands Crimpste.

Canosan nods, and sprints down the stairs, reaching inside his robe to pull out a scroll. He the unfurls it and throws it open in front of him. The scroll unrolls fully in midair, allowing Canosan to jump as it begins to release a glowing light. Once he vanishes, the scroll disappears behind him, leaving the courtyard empty.

Suddenly, within the depths of the temple inside the camp, the scroll reappears inside an empty hallway lit faintly by torches. It unrolls as it brightens the space, magical energy exploding from the letters. Canosan jumps out from the fabric and back onto the damp ground, the scroll rolling up and snapping into his hand. He places it back inside his robe before turning to catch sight of an open doorway, hidden by a cloth along a rope of silvery thread. Canosan walks over to it, ripping back the curtain to reveal what is inside the room.

A man of bones with wirey locks shifting in the wind, his cold blue eyes staring at the papers on the desk. His skeletal hands tapping on its surface, his bare ribs pulse up and down. As he sits behind a makeshift desk, his skeletal hands fall flat against a piece of parchment. Channeling magic into the grains, Scurge pauses at Canosan's intrusion.

"Excuse me Scurge but, the master requires your services," Canosan says, making his way into the room. Around them open scrolls cover the stone walls, the magic glowing brightly. Extending to the bottom of the room, they fall shy of the wooden bed in the center.

Scurge cracks his knuckles, closing the scrolls and allowing them to wrap around a copper pin hanging from the roof. He looks back at Canosan. "You'll find the scroll in there." He points Canosan over to a wooden dresser by the side of a giant window.

As Canosan steps toward it, a faint green glow emanates from the keyhole. Canosan opens the drawer and reaches inside with both hands, grabbing hold of the scroll as the glowing intensifies. "Come, let us not make the master wait any longer." He turns to the door.

Scurge nods, walking out behind him as both pull scrolls from within their robes. They both jump simultaneously into the scrolls, disappearing from the temple hall and reappearing at the top of the wall near where the others wait. Unrolling themselves, Scurge and Canosan jump out from the parchment and land against the cold top of the wall.

"We need to use the scroll to look out there," Crimpste says, pointing out into the distance.

Scurge snatches the scroll from Canosan, causing the scroll to shine brighter with his touch. He then walks over to the rail and unrolls the scroll outward, a magical eye popping out of it. The eye gazes out upon the land, Scurge's eyes beginning to glow bright green.

"Okay I see...." He then gasps, seeing two hurt mages running for their lives. Looking deeper, Scurge catches sight of a squad of warriors with glistening armor chasing them. Breaking the spell, he turns to Crimpste.

"What is it?" Crimpste asks urgently.

"We must help them, there are two mages and they don't stand a chance," Scurge replies quickly.

Crimpste turns to the other mages. "Don't just stand there! Everyone grab your cowls and scrolls, we have incoming!"

As the mages scramble to their places, Crimpste snatches his wand up with a tight fist. He storms down the walkway with Apocol and another man of similar build. His hood struggles to cover his white hair as it sneaks from under the rim, and the man quickens his pace as he comes toward Crimpste.

"What is Robilard?" Crimpste asks.

"Those damn Barazuls never learn," Robilard replies.

Crimpste joins the troop of mages as the final one pulls his cowl over his head. He looks at the mages standing silently before him, trying to figure out the next step of the plan. He turns to Robilard, who stands at the end of the line in his grayish robe. "Robilard, take five men up to the top and prepare for battle."

"Brothers, to the wall," Robilard commands pointing his wand to the staircase.

Crimpste then turns his attention to Apocol, who digs in his satchel for something. "Gather your own troops and don't allow those Barazul scum to enter this camp."

Apocol nods before walking over to the gate with a handful of troops in tow.

Crimpste watches as Robilard's troops begin to teleport to the top of the wall, while Apocol's troops take their position along the camp's main gate. Crimpste, now alone in the shadow the courtyard, takes a moment to gather his thoughts. He draws a deep breath before quickly ascending to the top of the wall, seeing the mages on guard and ready for action. Looking up the road, Crimpste sees the mages below fighting for their lives, becoming weaker with each passing second. Using up their final ounces of strength, the mages cast desperate spells, trying to throw off their pursuers.

Crimpste leans forward, looking to Robilard. "Begin your assault...NOW!"

Robilard turns to his troops as their hands flex around the handles of their scroll case. "You two," he commands, "provide a distraction. The rest focus on these intruders."

The mages open their cases, revealing the jumble of scrolls inside.

Crimpste looks down to Apocol, who waits patiently for his signal. "Keep them away from the gate," he commands.

"Canosan and Shlippmack, this is the time to use that new spell you talk about so much," Apocol says, watching as the other mages get into position. The two scurry towards him, smirks on their faces.

"Wait, Apocol, use this on them," Crimpste calls, reaching beneath a fold in his robe, pulling out two vials. Within each, a smoky, greenish liquid bubbles away, threatening to escape from its confines. He tosses them down to Apocol, who catches them both easily. "Those should replenish their strength."

Apocol looks down at the vials before handing one to both Canosan and Shlippmack. "Down the hatch, ladies," he says snarkily. He watches as the two men stare at the swishing liquid.

They slowly turn to each other before raising the vials to their mouth and drinking it with little hesitation. After they down the last drop, their eyes begin to water and their hands shake violently, their bodies starting to glow. They both tremble fiercely for a moment before the glowing fades away and both men fall to a knee.

Apocol looks over at Canosan as his skin gains a bluish tint before he rises back to his feet. Canosan's eyes flash open, now ice-blue, his breaths frosty as he exhales. Shlippmack rises to his feet as well, his eyes ablaze with fire, a magical flame engulfing his hands. The two mages turn to each other, chuckling at their newly given strength before turning back towards the gate and digging their heels in as the energy continues to consume them.

Crimpste looks down from the corner of his eyes, grinning as he watches as their power continue to strengthen. "Now we're ready for the attackers." He turns back to Robilard to observe the progress at the other front. Spotting the two mages standing in the spots, he watches as both grab handfuls of scrolls, preparing for battle. Both mages begin to run their fingertips over the glowing writing, and then raise their hands towards the sky, the weather beginning to turn. From out of their hands, magic channels up into the sky, creating enormous clouds that darken with each passing moment. As the clouds swell with moisture, the temperature drops suddenly, the air around them starting to freeze. The two mages' hands begin to turn icy, their skin frosting over. The clouds begin to rain down ice shards the size of great swords, surrounding the attackers.

Crempste watches as the attackers dodge their way through the falling ice. He turns to Robilard. "FIRE!"

Robilard motions to the mages who turn their scrolls sideways, each infusing with a different natural energy.

Crimpste looks down to Apocol and points toward the wooden gate.

Apocol signals Canosan and Shlippmack.

They each grab one of the handles and pull open the gate as rumbling starts to fill the air. As the rumbling stops, the opening widens, revealing the oncoming figures heading towards them. Apocol watches as the exhausted and wounded mages make their way inside the camp while their attackers approach the camp, defending against the onslaught from the mages on the wall.

Once they were safely inside, Canosan and Shlippmack release their sides of the door before running back to the others with scrolls in hand.

Crimpste watches as the mages' scrolls start to shed larger chunks of material as the magic level diminishes. The mages begin to reach inside their robes, pulling out wooden wands and aiming them down onto the road.

"We have them!" a voice yells.

Crimpste glances down to see the door shut, and the two injured mages safely inside. He then looks over to the intruders as they start to surround the camp's door.

Villianous human beings, the intruders hide their bare skin beneath metallic armor and linen shirts that reveal no opening between the armor's plates. Their gauntelts, covered in rivets for added protection, wrap around glinting swords that extend high above their helmets.

Furious, the intruders lift their iron shields from off their backs and place between themselves and the falling projectiles. Even as they struggle to brace themselves from the impact, they continue to unleash strikes upon the wooden barrier as it chips away. With the mages watching on, the attackers pause their strikes as the final thunder rumbles and the clouds lessen. The blue sky reveals itself and they turn their focus toward the door and drop their shields down onto the dirt path. Placing both hands onto the grip of their weapons, the attacks continue, sending larger chunks of woods into the ground.

Looking around at the drained mages surrounding him, Crimpste watches angrily as the door begins to splinter. Suddenly, the sky above clears allowing the intruders to strike with more ferocity. Crimpste's eyes widen as he runs towards the edge of the walkway, just shy of the gate. As he reaches the final stone, he leaps, spinning around and throwing down a scroll wrapped in chains of ice. He watches it explode on impact, unleashing a tidal wave of ice onto their enemies.

Catching them by surprise, the wave crashes onto two of them, freezing them instantly as the others dive into the shrubs nearby. Crimpste turns his attention to the walkway on the other side as he falls back to the ground. Noticing a small ledge in the wall, he manages to grasp it and pull himself up onto the walkway, where he watches them scramble away into the trees with their frozen comrades over their shoulders. Crimpste stands to watch their movement through the trees as they get farther away. He then turns back down to find the others gathering around the two hurt mages.

"Robilard," he commands, "you and Apocol take them down to the clinic for healings."

The other mages celebrate their victory as they surround the mages struggling to catch a breath in the center. The crowd quiets as Robilard and Apocol lead them down the path toward the doorstep of the building.

After they get safely inside, Crimpste leans on the stone railing, staring out into the sunset. He stares as a mixture of confusion and relief wash over his face, knowing mage brothers are safe behind the wall.

Canosan steps out from one of the larger buildings and makes his way toward his master. "Master Crimpste, is everything alright?"

"I am uncertain, young mage. I remember nothing of sending mages outside of this camp," Crimpste says, looking over at Canosan.

"What are you trying to say?" Canosan asks as he leans on a burnt wooden post in the center of the railing.

"I'm not sure. Please keep your guard up for any trouble," Crimpste replies, as he straightens.

"Yes, Master Crimpste," Canosan replies, watching him walk down the stairs.

"I must head into my chamber for some rest," Crimpste says as he glances back at Canosan, who bows slightly in response. He turns back, walking past the main building, seeing Robilard and Apocol walk outside. "How are they?"

"They're resting comfortably sir. It doesn't seem they were hurt too badly," Apocol replies.

"Glad to hear it," Crimpste says before continuing past them towards his chambers. He disappears inside the doorway, leaving Robilard and Apocol alone in the coming darkness.

They glance up at Canosan, seeing him standing guard, before turning away, catching sight of another mage sitting on a dusty barrel, drinking ale out of a canteen.

"Hey, Muertoz," Apocol calls.

Muertoz, the newest mage in the camp, lowers his canteen to his lap. He had been sent to their camp by Oriom Hill city guards for trying to start fires. "Is everything good?" he asks. Despite his rough beginning, he'd quickly become a friend to Robilard and Apocol.

"Not sure," Robilard replies. "Master Crimpste seems on edge about the battle."

"Of what?" Muertoz asks.

"The mages that we saved," Robilard replies.

"Maybe he's lightheaded from the crazy stunt he pulled," Apocol says, sitting down next to Muertoz and pulling a bottle of ale from his own bag.

The three laugh to themselves as they drink together and watch the night settle in around them. They lounge on the barrels for a while, surprised when suddenly the door to the main building flies open. The keeper rushes outside, a look of fear in his eyes as he turns towards them.

"Come quickly!" he gasps. "There is a commotion in the ward upstairs."

Apocol and Robilard jump up from the barrels, rushing inside with their wands in hand. They hear banging from the second floor, which grows louder as they make their way toward it.

Resting his hand on the rail, Apocol peeks up the stairs to try to get a better look of what was happening. "I command you to stop and report downstairs immediately," he calls.

After a second the commotion stops, and then suddenly a crash rings out, a body flying toward them. Looking down at their feet, Robilard and Apocol see a mage's body laying motionless, a bolt deep inside his ribcage. They run up to the stairway, watching as two beings make their way towards them. They realize they are the mages that had been rescued, now wearing full animal-armor. One places a crossbow along the fur on his back as they begin to laugh. The other one reaches into one of his pockets, pulling out a crystal, a trail of smoke swirling behind it.

Below, having heard the commotion, Crimpste tries to rush into the building, spotting the dead mage. He is surprised when the keeper suddenly steps in front of him, keeping him from going further. "I command you to leave me be," Crimpste yells, attempting to break the keeper's grasp.

"I'm sorry, sir, but I can't let you do that," the keeper replies, struggling to keep Crimpste from running up the stairs.

Defeated, Crempste takes a step back as the keeper remains in his path. He turns his eyes to the pile of bones. He sees Apocol and Robilard on the stairs, Robilard facing off with the intruders while Apocol stares down at the skeleton. "Do you recognize the skeleton?" he calls.

"It's Scurge," Apocol replies, pulling out his wand before pointing it at their enemies.

"Are you sure?" Crimpste asks, once again trying to step past the keeper. Crimpste stops, rage filling him.

The two intruders begin to descend the stairs with smirks on their faces. Apocol and Robilard back toward Crimpste, their eyes following the intruders. The two pause as they arrive at Scurge's body lying halfway on the last step. One of them then kneels and grabs the bolt in his hand, ripping it out of Scurge's ribcage. He grins slightly as he wipes the flesh from the shaft of the bolt. He places it carefully back into a pouch before following his comrade toward the door.

Crimpste, Apocol, and Robilard back into the courtyard, each on guard as the intruders step into the night air. Apocol and Robilard keep their wands raised, preparing for any sign of an attack. They watch mutely as one of the intruders lifts his hand, the crystal facing his body. The crystal's light starts to fluctuate, its glow engulfing the mage in a magical cloud. The cloud quickly fades, revealing a Barazul warrior hiding beneath the mage facade. The two Barazuls prepare to fight, when suddenly whistling noises split the air.

Crimpste and the others look up, seeing a hail of arrows darkening the moonlight.

"Run for cover!" Crimpste yells, watching as the onlooking mages around them begin to scatter. As the arrows fall, they strike down some of the mages before they can find safety.

A loud rumbling suddenly begins to fill the camp. Before Crimpste can do anything, the main gate suddenly explodes, showering the courtyard with debris. The explosion launches some of the mages into the air, throwing them against the buildings and barrels of supplies. A swarm of Barazul begin to charge the camp from out of the smoke.

Crimpste quickly turns to the other mages as they reach inside for their scrolls and wands. "This is where we bring back the peace back to our camp."

The mages gather up and turn towards the Barazul with their scrolls tight in their hands. As the Barazul rush into the camp with weapons and torches, the scrolls dissolve, allowing the magic to flow freely. Just as they get come within range, the mages fire off blasts of magic. Seizing on the distraction, the two Barazul that had snuck into the camp flee into the night.

Striking down a Barazul, Crimpste turns to the mages near him as the invading Barazul move into a defensive position against the magical onslaught. "Initiate escape plan C."

The mages turn to one another with a slight grin, knowing the signal. They turn to their opposition and fire off a single blast in their direction. Hitting them, the magic strips them of their weapons and armor, leaving them in a state of paralysis for the mages to attack. As they stand there, frozen in place, the mages begin to laugh hysterically.

"Silence, now grab what is important to you and then we shall—" Crimpste gasps in surprise when one of the warriors regains movement and charges at him. He turns around and snaps his fingers, transforming the warrior into a chicken.

"How did you do that?" Canosan asks, watching as the chicken-warrior strutted around in confusion.

"Pay attention to the scrolls I give you to study," Crimpste replies.

"I didn't make it to that chapter," Canosan says, looking down in shame.

"Now, as I was saying before I was so rudely interrupted, we need to escape now while we have the chance," Crimpste says. "Gather your things quickly." He watches as the mages gather their belongings before making their way back to Crimpste as he places scrolls into the folds of his robe. He turns around as the mages move toward the entrance, one by one teleporting to the main entrance on the other side of the frozen enemies. As they escape, Crimpste stops just outside of the camp, turning to look over his shoulder.

"What is it, sir?" Muertoz asks, pausing beside him.

"If they want our camp then they can have it in spirit," Crimpste answers.

"What's your plan?" Muertoz asks.

"Crusayder knows what to do," Crimpste replies, looking over to another mage that stepped in front of Muertoz.

Turning to the doorway, Crimpste watches as Crusayder makes his way over to the other end. They both raise their hands towards the doorway as the others look on. With their hands open, ice begins to shoot out from their fingertips into the fragments of the stone wall. Just as the final flakes solidify within the ice block, Crimpste turns towards the rest of the mages.

"Now, my brothers, let's really fire them up."

Crimpste watches as squads of mages make their way to the large trees along the border of the walls. They launch themselves upwards into the trees surrounding the camp as glowing spheres begin to appear through the leaves. As Crempste watches, fireballs launch from between the branches and over the wall.

Inside the camp, the Barazul's hands break free, the rest of their bodies following suit. They look around in disbelief, finding no trace of the mages, their weapons on the ground. Dispersing to gather their wits, they look all about as silence overtakes the clanging of their metal armor. With their swords back in their hands, they spin about until suddenly their eyes catch sight of the frozen block connecting the two sections of wall. Charging the door, they stop suddenly when streams of light dart along the floor, catching their attention. Looking up, they watch as fireballs begin to strike the buildings, instantly engulfing them in a blaze. As the camp floods with flames, the warriors charge the wall, unleashing strikes at every angle against the icy barrier.

The six mages stand at the foot of the burning camp as the Barazul's dying roars fill the night. They walk towards a barn sitting in a field nearby, hearing the crackling of flames as it overtakes the last whimper of the dying. Walking inside, Crimpste and Crusayder look back at the camp, catching sight of the faint reddish smoke streaming into the sky. They enter the barn with a sigh of relief, seeing their horses still puttering in their stalls.

"We shall stay here the night and then make our way to Dapalos," Crimpste says. He watches as the weary group beds down in the stalls alongside their horses. After making a makeshift bed in the hay, Crimpste eases down into it, closing his eyes.

Chapter Three

The night passes into day and Crimpste opens his eyes, stretching leasurely before standing on his feet. He opens the stable door and proceeds to wake up the others, starting with Canosan sleeping by the foot of his horse. One by one, the mages wake up as Crimpste continues along the row. Once they are all awake, the mages prepare for the day and begin to load up their horses. Before long, the mages mount up in their saddles, grabbing the reins and turning their horses toward the stone road. As the group assembles to leave, they shift their attention momentarily in the direction of their campsite.

With an ounce of sorrow, Crimpste and the other mages ride toward the gaping hole that was once where the door stood. The smell of charred remains fills the air as ash heavily coats the cracking walls. The group stops at the entrance, a mixture of emotions overcoming them. Their eyes water as they find the once clean courtyard to be covered completely in rubble. Along with mounds of ash, skeletal remains lay all over the floor, the smell of burnt flesh and the sound of crackling fire suffocating their senses.

Crimpste jumps off his horse, and turns toward the other mages, looking at the destruction. "I'm going to check what remains of my quarters. Salvage what you can."

The mages dismount as Crimpste walks up the path toward his open doorway. He places his hand onto the side of the wall, sliding it down to wipe away the ash, sorrow filling him. Inside, the room is a shell of its former self, with furniture broken into pieces along with mounds of dust. Stepping on a dying ember, Crimpste makes his way into the center of the room. His eyes shift over all the debris laying before him as he turns toward a large case sitting along the wall. Despite being charred from the flames, the lid remains shut, protecting the scrolls.

Crimpste walks over and pulls open the door, which unseals with a flourish of magic. He reaches inside the mound of scrolls and pulls out a scroll with a golden thread wrapped around it. As he looks at it, he drops the scroll onto the ground watching as it dissipates and blows away in the tiniest breeze. He leaves his former quarters, shaking his head. Before him, the others have gathered what supplies could be found and are waiting for him on their horses.

He mounts up as well, grabbing the reins and urging his horse towards the entrance. "Come, Brothers, let us ride to Dapalos."

Riding steadily away from the camp, they push forward through the stretch of land just beyond the thick trees, the sun shifting across the sky overhead. About midday, they crest a rising hill, their eyes catching sight of the remains of an old shade tree. The group surrounds the tree in the shadier sections to allow their horse to take a breath. They get off their horses as each mage reaches into one of their saddlebags to pull out food they had stashed away. As they eat, they catch sight of traveling herds of animals.

"What do we intend to do in Dapalos?" Shlippmack asks, wiping his mouth as he looks over at Crimpste.

Crimpste looks at the group as they all turn toward him, anxiously awaiting a reply. "We will meet with the Elders and demand action."

Muertoz place his back against the fragile trunk as he lowers his chunk of bread down to his lap. "Are you sure they will even know the proper retaliation?" He is greeted with glares as Crimpste turns his head.

"You watch your tongue," Shlippmack says angrily.

"I truly hope so, young mage," Crimpste replies, waving Shlippmack down. "Otherwise they wouldn't be the leaders of the Minazue." He watches as Muertoz nods, locking his fingers behind his head.

"We just need to focus on the task at hand," Crusayder says from the other end of the group. "Mourn the brothers we have lost and move forward." One by one, the rest of the group nod their heads in agreement.

Once finished with his meal, Crimpste walks over to his horse. "Mount up," he says, pulling himself onto his horse. "We have far to go still."

Leaving the tree in their dust, the sky turns cloudy, the air thickening with moisture as they charge down the road towards the Eternos line.

"There is a farm up ahead that can provide us haven," Crimpste says, pointing toward an area around a mountainous hill.

The mages follow him down a pathway, kicking up mud as they pass a sign, *Thorloc Manor: Minazue Welcome.* Continuing down the road, their eyes catch sight of a home in the shadows of the hillside. As they near, it is plain to see paint peeling off, the drizzle clanging on the makeshift roof. As they arrive at the front door, Canosan looks over at the window, seeing the curtains shift inside. Before they can dismount, the door to the house creaks open, revealing a massive green orc standing in the doorway.

Crimpste begins to smile, sliding from his horse. "Hello old friend, never thought I'd see you again," he says, making his way up the stairs separating the ground from the wooden patio.

"I didn't know that he had orc friends," Shlippmack whispers as he looks over to Muertoz.

"It looks like he does," Muertoz replies with a shrug as he turns his attention back to Crimpste.

The orc lets out a chuckle from behind his lines of sharp teeth. Once under the roof, Crimpste and the orc greet one another with a handshake.

"Master, is this beast a friend?" Shlippmack asks, his horse shifting uncomfortably underneath him.

The orc looks over Crimpste's shoulder, meeting Shlippmack' eyes. "You watch your tongue mage, or I shall crush your skull," the orc replies, revealing his top teeth, dripping with saliva.

"This is Raeloc Talon," Crimpste says, placing his hand up against Raeloc's chest. "He's a former member of the Elite Guard in Dapalos."

"Aye, and I've known your leader since he himself was a mere apprentice," Raeloc says, shifting his sight to Crimpste.

The group gasps as they turn to Crimpste in disbelief as he nods his head in agreement.

"We are in need of shelter. Would you allow us to spend the night in your farmhouse, for old time's sake?" Crimpste asks.

"Certainly, but I do have one question," Raeloc replies.

"Ask away," says Crimpste, tilting his head.

"What happened to the camp I heard you were leading?" Raeloc asks as Crimpste looks back at the others.

"That, my friend, is a long story which I will tell you, over a bottle of your famous brew," Crimpste replies with a grin, pointing over to the fireplace beyond the open doorway.

"That sounds like a fair deal," Raeloc says, returning his grin and bowing as he motions them inside. He then watches as the dozen mages turn their attention toward a barn nearby as shadows sneak out from the torch light within.

As the mages bed their mounts down in a creaking barn nearby, Crimpste follows Raeloc inside the house. Soon everyone gathers, the group taking seats around a wooden table as mugs sit in front of them. They visibly relax as they lift the brown liquid to their mouths, clearly relieved to be in a safe place. As they drink, Crimpste tells Raeloc of the attack on the camp.

"We thought we were safe as peace briefly returned when a crash broke down our shields," Crimpste says in a low somber tone. Looking around at the others, Crimpste watches his brothers as they shut their eyes. Laying their heads back against the pillows of hay around the room, Crimpste turns to Raeloc as he takes a sip of grog.

"Did you not suspect anything?" Raeloc asks, placing his mug inside a ring of moisture on the table.

"Unfortunately no, thanks to that damn magical orb in his possession," Crimpste replies, his hand tightening its grip around his mug.

"How did you guys get away?" Raeloc asks, watching Crimpste relax his hand as he lifts it away.

"We transformed them into pathetic creatures, giving us time to escape with our magic," Crimpste says, gathering himself out of his chair. He finds a space on a chair in the corner of the room, just outside the glow from the fireplace. Taking a seat, Crimpste places his head against the chair's cushion before gently shutting his eyes as his breathing softens.

"Kloza will surely want to hear about this treachery," Raeloc snarls as he turns his head toward the peaceful night sky. As the silent night passes toward the arrival of the sun, the horizon explodes with spears of light that pierce the musty darkness inside the room. Out from the side, Raeloc appears from the shadows as Crimpste is the first to open his eyes.

"Good morning old friend," Crimpste says softly before releasing a mighty yawn.

"Morning, please enjoy the rations of bread and fresh water from the springs along the hillside," Raeloc replies.

Crimpste shifts his sight as the other mages around the room awaken. He then heads over to the table, grabbing a slice of bread as the others sit up from the places. Seeing the growing light outside, Crimpste scarfs down the food and makes his way toward the door. Opening it wide, the door swings open, sending a gush of fresh air into the room as the mages rise and head toward the assortment of bread chunks. As they gather up some breakfast, Crimpste heads outside as his shadow disappears from the back wall.

The other follow his lead, stepping away from the table and making their way outside. Once the final one was outside, Crimpste reappears in the doorway before pausing as he sees Raeloc approach the table.

"Farewell, good friend, and thanks again for the drink," he says, waving farewell.

He turns to find Canosan bringing his horse to the edge of the patio. Raeloc stands in the doorway with his hand pressing against a bending post, watching his friend climb onto his horse. One by one, the mages pass him by to say their farewells before making their way back down the path. Once the final mage was within the beams of sunlight, Raeloc leans against the post, turning his attention to a tree nearby as the final leaves blow off.

✳✳✳

It is late in the day when finally the mages arrive at the border into Eternos, and their eventual destination. After a while, Crimpste looks upwards as the light begins to fade, allowing night to creep over the landscape. He looks around at the others, seeing how exhausted they are.

"We're not far now," he says to his comrades, pointing into the distance. A watchtower can be seen on the darkening horizon.

The mages seem to perk up as they ride closer, a Minazue flag waving down from its post. Coming closer, the group spots a mage through a tower window, his palms downward and greenish energy seeping into his body from a magic scroll. With each wave of magnificent energy, different and colorful glows resonate against the mage's skin. They watch as the light suddenly disappears and the magic returns to the scrolls, leaving the mage in darkness.

Crimpste turns toward Canosan and Shlippmack. "You two, get off and check out what he was doing in there," he says.

Canosan and Shlippmack dismount, hesitantly walking over to the window while the rest look on. When they arrive at the window, they peak inside and are in shock to find the room completely empty, not even a scroll on the ground. In disbelief, the two turn to Crimpste.

"He's gone," they whisper.

Confusion fills Crimpste as he looks inside the window, seeing the mage clearly in view. "I don't care how scary you think he is, I command you to look in there," he snaps, pointing back at the window.

Canosan and Shlippmack turn back toward the window, and to their astonishment see the mage pouring a bubbling blue liquid into a vial, shining like a diamond. The mage stops and places the vial back on the table as he turns towards an open spell book. Startled, Canosan and Shlippmack return to the group.

"Is he one of us?" Crimpste asks.

"Believe so, but couldn't really see anything beyond the glowing magic," Canosan replies, trying to calm his shaking hands.

Crimpste looks back at the window before dismounting his horse. He walks over to the doorway and walks in, just as the mage starts to pour another liquid inside the one within the vial. At his intrusion, the mage slams the containers onto the table in surprise, his eyes shifting to Crimpste.

"Pardon my interruption, I require your services," Crimpste says, examining the room.

The mage steps into the light of a fireplace, revealing a face covered with scars and a faded and torn robe. "Welcome to the Jade Eye Inn," he says. "My name is Lozari."

"Greetings, I am Crimpste," he says. He motions to the magic items on the table. "May I ask what you are doing here?"

"I'm preparing spells to repeal any demonic curse or spell," Lozari replies, grabbing hold of the vial and placing it on top of a piece of shelving.

"That truly sounds like a daunting task," Crimpste replies. He walks over to the window and looks out, seeing the other mages waiting for him.

"Do you need a place to stay?" asks Lozari as he spots the mages over Crimpste's shoulder.

"That would certainly be helpful," Crimpste replies as Lozari nods his head.

"I think I can help you with that. Just give me a moment," Lozari says. He walks over to his spell book as he begins to flip through the pages.

"What are you searching for?" Crimpste asks, watching as Lozari's hand stops after flipping another page.

"Found it," Lozari replies, smiling as he points down at one of the yellowish pages. He looks down as he places his hand over the page and begins to mumble the words written on it. As he speaks the words, them begin to lift from the page and float up from the book and into his hand, leaving the page blank. Once the final word is gone, his hand begins to glow and his body begins to fade. Crimpste watches as Lozari's body replicates, a new Lozari standing on either side of him.

"Tell the cranky orc we have guests who require a night's sleep," Lozari says, looking over to the one on his left.

It then nods its head and begins to walk towards the door, vanishing out of sight. After a moment, there is a crash and then a series of rumblings within the earth. Moments later, a massive creature with brownish skin appears, an axe in his hand with a rage in his eyes.

At the sight of the beast, the mages outside scatter, leaping into the shadows to hide. Deciding on an attack plan, two of the mages erupt from the darkness and grab hold of the orc's massive arms as Crusayder gets in front, struggling to hold his sword steady. The orc looks at the two holding its arms, smirking as he shakes his head in disbelief. He turns his attention to Lozari before flinging the mages onto the ground and turning to Crusayder. He grabs hold of him and tosses him over a fence, into the nearby pigpen. The orc then watches as Crusayder stumbles to his feet, struggling to wipe the mud from his robe. The other mages turn towards him, grinning at his misfortune before pulling out their swords and facing the orc.

Before the action can intensify, Lozari raises his hands. "It's okay!" he yells. "This is Grozok, my protector."

Grozok snarls, and then places his axe back into its holder as the mages slowly place their swords away. "The next time you send one of your damn clones to me unannounced, I'm going to slice it and you in half," Grozok snarls toothily.

"I've got to keep you on your toes for any real threat," Lozari smirks. "But for now, we have company and they require a place to sleep."

Grozok snarls once more as he charges up to Lozari, grabbing him by his neck as he slams him up against the wall. "How's this for on my toes?"

The mages turn towards each other and then to Crimpste as he looks on with his arms hanging to his side. He walks toward Grozok as he clears his throat. "Evening Grozok, my name is Crimpste and I'm the leader of this band of mages."

Grozok places Lozari back on the ground before turning his intimidating glare toward him. "Why is a bunch of mages here and not at their camp?" Grozok asks, regaining his composure as Lozari takes a step back.

"We were attacked by a group of warriors," Crimpste replies.

"That does explain the orange glow in last night's sky," Grozok says, rubbing the loose hairs on his chin.

"Must have been from our fireworks," Shlippmack replies, darting his eyes across the room.

"Well, if you want a place to stay we have some hammocks up on the next level," Grozok continues, pointing his massive hand out the open doorway.

"That sounds just fine," Crimpste replies.

Grozok turns to lead the way outside. They follow him up and around the side of the tower, where he stops and points to the raggedy rope hammocks that were molding into the poles. Connecting the ropes to the foundation is a large animal bone protruding from the pillar. Each mage makes their way over to a hammock, struggling to get comfortable as Grozok watches on from the ramp to the third level. As most attempt to lie down, Crimpste looks over at Grozok leaning on one of the poles.

"Please keep us safe from the dangers of the night," Crimpste says, resting his sword against the pole beneath his hammock.

"I will do my best," Grozok says as he walks up the ramp and then out of view.

Crimpste turns to look at his brothers who fall asleep quickly with their hands beneath their heads. He then turns his attention back to the star lit sky and shuts his eyes to enjoy the peace of the night.

Chapter Four

Inside a castle in the heart of the Barazul capital, Athial, stands the leader of the Barazul, King Galaxi Ronos. He is of human body with blonde hair falling over his forehead and neck. His red eyes strike fear in all that had seen it, one of which hides beneath a patch from the great war that had torn the two tribes apart. Wearing only the finest armor, his body molds around the metals on his chest plate as a golden crown sits on his head. From the center of each shoulder piece a ruby glows to match his death-wielding blade. King Ronos looks up from a parchment paper that reveals the mages location, looking at the sorcerer in front of him.

"That is enough, Sorcerer; I have seen enough of this," King Ronos says, turning to the chamber door.

The sorcerer waves his hand underneath the sleeve of his robe over the parchment, distorting it and removing the image altogether. The sorcerer, from behind the cowl of his robe, looks back to King Ronos as he stands statuesque in the middle of the doorway. "The deed is done Sire, what are your orders for them now?"

King Ronos stops in front of the door and looks over his shoulder at the Sorcerer with an evil smirk. "Nothing. Let them go to Dapalos. They shall find that similar fates have been dealt."

"Understood, Master," the sorcerer replies as he walks through the side doorway.

King Ronos turns his attention to the chamber door, shoving it open with the smirk still on his face. The door opens into the throne room where his two consuls wait for his arrival. On one side is King Golos Hinnerog from the Frozen Hills: short stature and heavy facial hair makes up his frame, as his greenish complexion combines into his silvery hair. His fingers and hands are frostbitten as they wrap around two twin axes that extend to the ground. The metal in his armor shimmers in the light as he then turns to look over at the other consul.

Opposite him is the beautifully powerful Elementia Vorrais. Elementia was unlike most, her slim physique hiding unmatched intelligence, wisdom that could bring down kingdoms. Her silk robe channels energy from the elements that surround her, her metallic-blue skin rising to her black hair as her piercing white eyes stare back at King Ronos.

King Ronos grins as he sits upon his golden throne atop a bright red carpet. "Thank you for coming, sorry for keeping you waiting."

"Have the Minazue forces been weakened?" Elementia Vorrais asks, stepping toward King Ronos.

"No, there has been a change of plans," King Ronos replies, his hands resting against the armrests of his chair as he leans back.

Golos Hinnerog stands next to Elementia Vorrais. "How dare you sit there doing nothing to stop them!" he snaps, the icicles in his hair wiggling dangerously with his rage.

"Don't get your gnomes in a bunch, Golos, I'm the leader," King Ronos replies darkly, sitting up in his chair.

Golos mumbles under his breath as he sits down on a bench nearby and reaches into his sack, pulling out a bottle of ale. Keeping his eyes on King Ronos, he raises the ale to his mouth, taking a swig from the bottle.

"So how, may I ask, do you have it under control?" Elementia asks, watching as Golos places the bottle next to him on the bench.

"We have knocked out some of the foothold without using much of our own army," King Ronos says with a menacing smile.

Suddenly, Golos spits some of the ale out in disbelief.

King Ronos looks down at the ale on the floor, and then turns his attention back to the two consuls. "While we wait for them to fail our forces continue to strengthen."

Elementia sits beside Golos, raising her hand to her face as she ponders the situation. "I would love to see Kolozi's face when he realizes that his mighty kingdom is crumbling."

"Oh no, but we're the Minazue, we're so mighty and powerful," Golos says mockingly. The three begin to laugh aloud, interrupted suddenly by a knock at the door.

"You may enter," King Ronos yells as the guards pull the doors open, allowing two humans to stumble inside the room. "Ah, if it's not the trade master and his apprentice to deliver today's fares." King Ronos looks over, grinning at the large sack that the two struggle to carry inside.

Elementia and Golos watch as they make their way over to King Ronos and place the brown bag at the foot of his throne. As it settles, the they turn to the king before bowing their heads as their knees hit the stone floor.

"Oh, Mighty King, we bring you today's trade fees, and the tax we charge in your name," the trade master says, struggling to keep his head toward the ground.

King Ronos sits up in his chair, reaching for the bag. "Today must have been busy. This one is heavier compared to the others you have brought."

"Yes, Sire, it was. Many came to do business in your market," the apprentice replies, struggling to keep his youthful confidence at bay.

Suddenly, King Ronos lifts his eyes up, and shoots them at the apprentice, who continues to kneel. "How dare a mere apprentice speak in front of the Barazul elders!" King Ronos yells, exploding from his throne, his guards approaching the apprentice.

"Please, Mighty King, spare him he is just a boy who knows no better," the trade master begs, turning his aging face toward his young apprentice.

"Never, this boy must be taught the rules of this kingdom," King Ronos commands, motioning the guards closer. He watches as they walk up to the boy and lift him to his feet before pushing him towards the door.

As the apprentice struggles to break free from their grasp, the trade master keeps still, ignoring his cries for help. The three elders watch as the guards drag the boy outside the chamber and King Ronos turns his attention back to the trade master as the screams fade to a whisper. "Now trade master, besides finding a more respectful apprentice, you must continue my tax on the goods that arrive."

"In your name," the trade master mumbles, keeping his head bowed.

King Ronos reaches into the bag, pulling some amber coins out from its depths. He looks over at the trade master, dropping the coins on the floor. "Now, quickly, gather these coins and leave my chamber immediately."

The trade master lifts his head to look at the coins and quickly gathers them up. Putting them away, he scurries over to the doorway, the door shutting behind him.

King Ronos then looks at the sack, and places it the edge of his lap. "Now what shall I do with this?" Receiving no response, King Ronos looks over to the others, seeing annoyance on their faces.

"Care to get rid of that distraction?" Elementia asks

"Excuse me a moment, will you?" King Ronos replies, looking over to the side room where the sorcerer places a scroll upon an empty shelf. King Ronos unleashes a deafening whistle, causing the sorcerer to stumble, nearly knocking off a pile of parchment.

At the king's beckoning, he jumps off the tiny ladder and walks out of the room, toward the king on his throne. "Yes Master, what do you require?"

"Take this to the vault for safe keeping," King Ronos says, handing the sack over to the sorcerer.

As the sorcerer reaches for the sack, it slips from his fingers and crashes to the floor, causing the sorcerer to look up in embarrassment. "Assist," the sorcerer mumbles, watching as the Barazul elders stare at him.

The room starts to quiver as a Marbula, a creature that is the definition of demonic, playing with chains of blood wrapped around its muscular frame, appears from out of the shadows. Its red eyes twitch about the room, catching sight of the bag sitting in front of the sorcerer's feet. It lifts the bag in its dripping hands and carries it, following the sorcerer out of the room.

Once they are gone, King Ronos turns back to the two consuls. "Was there anything else I need to tell you?"

"You brought us here saying you had amazing news in the Barazul quest to destroy the Minazue," Golos replies.

"Ah, yes, my scouts have come to me with news of a new Barazul ally," King Ronos says confidently as his fingers wrap around the golden handles of his chair.

Golos and Elementia turn to each other in disbelief before quickly turning back to King Ronos.

"Will this new ally you speak of help us counter the new powers of the Minazue?" Elementia asks.

"Stupid elves couldn't accept me as their leader," Golos grumbles, tightening his grip on his mug.

"Yeah, cause had they, you would have considered yourself the savior of the Barazul," Elementia replies.

"Whatever the case is, this group is known as the Lunarions, and they bring with them scrolls of the highest power," King Ronos replies.

"How are they able to use them?" Golos asks, taking a sip of his ale.

"Shanera," King Ronos says, causing the two to look at each other.

"Shanera, the sorcerer who can bring forth the power of nature?" Golos asks as Elementia Vorrais rubs her forehead.

"The very same, my dwarven friend. It will be like the Minazue came across an army of divine warriors," Elementia says.

"Blasted things wiping out so many of my brothers, they think it's so easy to kill anything below four feet tall," Golos says as he takes another swig.

Elementia rests a hand on his shoulder to comfort him. "It's okay Golos, we also want revenge on them after they drove us out of Nobiliad City," she says, watching as Golos loosens his grip around his drink.

"They shall pay!" Golos yells, causing the room to quake.

Elementia removes her arm from his shoulder and turns her attention to King Ronos, seeing him smirking at the crying Dwarf. "So when are we going to meet them?"

"They will be arriving at our steps shortly," says King Ronos.

As he tries to regain his composure, Golos looks towards King Ronos, who is smirking upon his throne. "Is there anything else you're not telling us before they get here?"

"I still am unsure of a lot myself, however, I can tell you their leader's name is Jadin," King Ronos says. Before the leaders can respond, a knock at the door interrupts the conversation.

"What is it the meaning of this disruption?" Scowling, King Ronos watches as the door cracks open a bit and a guard's head peeks inside.

"Pardon, but the Lunarion army has arrived in our waters," the guard says before disappearing back behind the door.

"I guess now is the time to find out," King Ronos replies.

The three get up and walk out of the chamber door one by one, gathering in the town square. Stepping from out of the diamond pillars, they make their way down the marble steps and onto the stone street. They turn their attention to the side of the building, where the watery sea merges with a wooden pier. Standing alongside a group of commoners, they watch as boats made of wood and seashells approach the dock. The boats anchor as the final boat stops between the others.

On board, Jadin stands tall over servants who pull the long paddles inside the boat. With his heavy armor blending like mud and sand, Jadin looks around as the double door opens. From out of the darkness, four Lunarion warriors, with their grayish complexion, step forward into the light. Revealing their heavy metal armors and bright weapons made with solid coral, they step around Jadin protectively. Jadin then steps off his platform and down onto the deck where he turns toward the gangway. He steps off the boat as the warriors stand close behind him. King Ronos walks over to him with his hand stretching out between them.

"Greetings Jadin, welcome to Athial, the heartland of the Barazul," King Ronos says as he leads Jadin towards his consuls. As they near Golos and Elementia, the crowd around them disburses.

"Who are the others?" Jaidin asks, shifting his glance between the two.

"Allow me to introduce you to Elementia Vorrais, and King Golos Hinnerog," King Ronos says as he points to them respectively.

As they bow to him in respect, Jadin turns to his warrior guards. "You may leave now, I have much to discuss with them," he commands. He turns to follow King Ronos.

As he leads the way back toward the castle, King Ronos smirks at the number of Lunarions making their way off the boat. "Thank you for bringing your men as well, they can surely aid us in the defeat of the Minazue," he says, turning his attention back to Jadin.

"It is our pleasure to aid in the defeat of the Minazue," Jadin says.

The four proceed to walk back to the main chamber, stirring up whispers from the servants and commoners as they pass. As they arrive at the stairs, a yell suddenly fills the street.

"Lord Hinnerog, I come bearing your stout per your request!" the voice echoes. They turn to see a gnome running towards them, carrying a bottle covered in various furs. As the gnome arrives at the foot of the stairs, he hands the bottle to Golos, who smiles as he takes it in his grasp.

"Thank you, Groag, for the stout, now you may go," Golos says, pointing out to the direction which Groag had come.

As they watch on, Groag turns around and runs off into the crowds of people in the square. Turning back around, Golos sees the others standing at the top of the stairs, waiting for him. Golos runs up the stairs, trying to open the bottle as his feet connect with each stair. Just as he gets to the group, the cap pops off, and he pauses, drinking the entire thing in one massive gulp. He then takes a step back and throws the empty bottle over the stone wall, sending it crashing to the outside.

Entering the chamber, the four find a table in the center of the room on top of a black silken rug. Each takes a seat, finding a single golden goblet waiting for them with the finest wine up to the brim.

"Now we can discuss the best location to wage this mighty battle," King Ronos says as he looks around the table.

Looking at one another in silence, Golos slaps the goblet off the table and onto the floor. "I say we fight them in the Valley of the Frozen Cinder! There the cold will snuff the flames of their torches bare!" Golos roars to the delight of Elementia.

"As I'm sure you're aware, most humans and Lunarions cannot adapt to such a harsh environment," Jadin says as he relaxes in his chair. Silence falls over the room as they wrack their brains.

"Volzia!" they suddenly yell, exploding from their chairs. Each stands with a grin as their chairs slam to the ground, sending an echo through the room.

"We shall prepare for battle at the Nomaz Crown, where the bones of the Minazue shall be swallowed up by the tides of the sand," King Ronos says, lifting his goblet off the table and into the sky. He watches as the others do the same in agreement.

"I say we stage the true battle in the Roa'Madi ruins," Jadin says, looking around at the others.

"My messenger at the Hinnerog encampment tells me it's a small area, great for a Barazul victory," Golos adds, looking over at Jadin.

King Ronos ponders this as he lowers his goblet before he raises it once more. "We shall defeat them at Roa'Madi."

"Victory for the Barazul!" the group yells in unison before bringing their goblets to their mouths.

Chapter Five

The next morning Crimpste opens his eyes, finding nothing but empty hammocks all around him. He quickly gathers his belongings, and rushes down the ramp, where he finds the other mages standing next to Grozok.

"Well, look who finally decided to join us," Muertoz says as he breaks off a piece of bread. Tossing it up to Crimpste, Muertoz watches him catch the bread, and eat it as he continues to walk toward the group.

Grozok gathers them altogether as Crimpste makes his way through the line of mages. "Well, now that we're all together, I can say on behalf of the Jade Eye, thank you for not setting anything a blaze," Grozok says.

"Is it because we wield the power of fire?" Muertoz asks.

"Nope, just the last time we housed someone they sneezed out a stream of fire which nearly burned down the forest," Grozok replies, pointing over to an area of brush.

The mages look over, seeing the leaves turned to ash, the grass beneath covered in a layer of soot. All the mages bow their gratitude to the orc, except for Crimpste, who simply nods his head. The mages then mount up on their horses, preparing for the day's ride. Once everything is together, they place their scrolls back inside their robes.

"Thank you, and now we set off for Dapalos," Crimpste says to Grozok, striking his horse, causing it to take off down the road.

The other mages do the same, following him toward the road

that connects Eternos with Zalzona. As they pull up to a line of dead tree trunks covering the edge of the land, Shlippmack stops and looks across the grass, seeing souls wandering through the trunks of the trees. Before fear can set in, Shlippmack catches up to the rest of the group, which continues onward down the road into Eternos. As the mages ride into Eternos, their eyes gaze around at the desolate land beyond the line of trees. The sandy ground beneath their feet quakes with energy as the remainder of Eternos struggles to keep the withering trees alive. Their horses stop momentarily, allowing them to look back over the road. Apocol takes this chance to catch up to Crimpste.

"According to my map, we are approaching a Minazue hold," Apocol says.

"I know where we are, just make sure you keep an eye on them," Crimpste says, pointing toward the cliffs.

Apocol turns his head, and spots a group beginning to gather near the horizon by a sinking lake. As the mages continue forward, large stone walls like their own camp come into view just beyond the first set of hills. Urging their mounts forward faster, they rise over the first hill, seeing the walls expanding in all directions. They admire the armor wall with its fragments of skeletons stuck all along the face. Cutting the road off abruptly, a massive gate stands in the center of the open valley. The group begins to ride faster toward it, three figures suddenly blocking the way.

The figure in the center is much larger than the others, with greenish skin and shiny metal armor. As they come closer, he raises his hand, halting the mages in their tracks. Crimpste and Apocol get off their horses as the rest remain still. They slowly walk toward him, seeing the guard scowl and cross his arms, the other two beside him standing at attention.

"Do you not recognize your friend?" Crimpste asks, inspecting the large orc as his teeth hang over his top lip. Without a reply, the two grunts pull out their axes, directing them at the approaching mages.

"I do not know anyone outside Minazue Hold," the orc replies, exhaling deeply as Crimpste looks on in disappointment. "Anyways, mage, what is your business here in the Hold?"

"Are you not Zalot Noroc, the first head guard of the Noroc group?" Crimpste asks as the orc's charcoal eyes focus harder on him.

"That is my name, but how would a simple outsider know that?" Zalot asks, confused.

"I am Master Crimpste, leader of the mages," Crimpste replies, spreading out his arms.

"I do remember a Crimpste, but why should I believe you are him and not some phony?" Zalot replies.

Apocol's eyes widen in disbelief as he pulls out his sword and aims it at one of the grunts.

Zalot's eyes quickly jump to him as Crimpste quickly steps in front of Apocol's blade.

"How dare you ask such an absurd question!" Apocol yells as he sticks his head out from behind Crimpste.

"Keep your calm. These are friends, not foes," Crimpste replies, glancing at Apocol.

As Zalot and the grunts watch on, laughter overtakes them as they point in the direction of the group.

"Look boys, the Barazul can't even find a way to deceive us without deceiving themselves," Zalot says in a chuckle.

"You dare call us Barazul? How do we know you aren't a Barazul yourself?" Apocol demands.

"Watch your tongue, boy, or I might just cut it out," Zalot yells as his grunts step forward with their hands upon their weapons.

"Bring it on, stupid orc!" Apocol yells, trying to charge forward.

Crimpste suddenly pushes him back toward the others as they dismount, preparing for a fight. "Enough of this!"

"I will have your Minazue mask for that, you dirty Barazul!" Zalot screams.

"Enough, Apocol put your sword away. There is no need for weapons," Crimpste says as Zalot begins to laugh again. He looks at Zalot. "We are not Barazul and we do not wish to fight."

"I'm so scared at the thought of what the mighty Barazul will do to me," Zalot says, shaking his hands in mockery.

Crimpste quickly turns towards Zalot as Apocol hesitantly steps back to the others.

"The Barazul can do nothing, but I, Master Crimpste, can do

something," he replies as his hands begins erupt in a magical flame.

"Oh, and what would that be?" Zalot asks as he keeps the tip of his sword facing Crimpste.

"Well, I came prepared in case you didn't let us pass," Crimpste replies, the flames fading away as he reaches inside one of the folds in his robe.

The grunts, without hesitation, grasp their axe handles tightly as they watch Crimpste pull out a scroll. Suddenly, Crimpste tosses the scroll at Zalot, who catches it, dropping his sword onto the ground.

Zalot looks at the scroll, and his eyes begin to widen, spotting the mage insignia on its band.

"What is it?" one of the grunts asks, watching Zalot carefully.

Ignoring the question, Zalot unrolls the scroll and begins to read it as Crimpste looks on with a smirk. After reading the last line of text, he rolls it back up and then looks back at the grunts. "This document confirms his identity."

"Which is what exactly?" the grunt asks, causing his counter-part and Zalot to look over at him.

"Crimpste, leader of the lone Minazue mage camp," Crimpste replies, watching as the they turn their attention over to him.

"Yes, so you see, you have been threatening the leader of the mages!" Apocol yells from behind Crimpste.

"Now you grunts, put those axes down," Zalot yells, smacking down their swords with his axe before dropping his back to the ground. As they put their swords away, Zalot looks over at Crimpste, extending his hand out. "Greetings, my friend."

"Greetings," Crimpste replies before reaching out and shaking hands.

"I'm sorry for the inconvenience, however Minazue Hold is on high alert," Zalot says, letting go of Crimpste's hand.

"That is understandable. We, too, have been attacked by the enemy," Crimpste replies as he steps back toward Apocol.

"Well then, let me formally welcome you to Minazue Hold," Zalot says as he and the two grunts move to the side, allowing the mages to see the open gateway waiting for them.

In front of their eyes, a wall stands tall as archer sentries pace back and forth along the top. Inside, citizens dash back and forth into the pavilions around the central stone castle. Its stone exterior is solid, revealing its smooth exterior with bright red carpeting ending just shy of the sandy road. The mages look among one another, watching as Crimpste and Apocol grab hold of their horse's reins. Walking them forward, Zalot bows as they pass, the grunts stumbling around before bowing next to him. As the mages enter the camp with their horses behind them, they pass through a market road, their eyes catching sight of a barn made of debris from the wasteland nearby. Once inside, they pass through the stalls, finding each one to be occupied by horses of a variety of colors.

Finally, Crimpste pushes out the large back door, finding himself outside in a designated pasture area. Releasing hold of his horse, he watches as the horse gallops off into the grass before nibbling away. The rest of the mages do the same, allowing their horses to follow the other into the field. As the dust settles, the group turns toward a door in the fence line and then watch as Crimpste opens the door ahead of them. One by one, the mages make their way out of the pasture as the last one through locks the door in place.

They turn their attention to the castle in the center as the light cascades from out of the hallway. Making their way forward, they turn into the open doorway before following Crimpste inside. Once inside, the mages observe the rows of torches unlit on both sides as wooden chandeliers hang from above, lighting the way. Continuing down, the hall opens, revealing a couple of tables of sentries enjoying their meal of bread and meat. Catching sight of the mages, they drop their food as the mages continue forward through another doorway.

This time the mages find themselves in an exquisite room with paintings along each wall as tables pivot magically in every corner. The floor is carpeting made from cooled volcanic stones which sparkles with gems that have been deemed unworthy for any other use. Above their heads, chandeliers made of animal bones cause the shadows to retreat, pouring light into the corners of the room. In the middle of the room the mages find Zalot standing next to another human figure. His ears pointing upwards, the man keeps his piercing red eyes upon the group. Black hair drips behind both ears and onto his metal chest plate.

"Who is this?" Crimpste asks.

"This is Dironte," Zalot says, turning his attention to Dironte as he bows his head.

"I'm the leader of the Minazue Guardians, which keep this town safe from all dangers," Dironte replies as the guards around the room roar in unison.

"My name is Crimpste and this is my group of mage brothers," Crimpste says as the room silences.

"Well then, let me welcome you to our home," Dironte replies. He turns to Zalot and kneels before making his way toward an open seat among the guards, leaving the group alone with Zalot.

Zalot turns to the group with a smirk, watching as the mages continue to look around the room. "He's a man of a few words."

Crimpste nods his head at him before turning back to Canosan, seeing him trailing a couple of steps behind the rest of the group. "What are you doing Canosan?"

"Nothing, sir, just resting against the wall," Canosan replies, adjusting his hands between his head and the wooden post. The weariness is evident in all the mages faces.

"So, what brings you here to Minazue Hold?" Zalot asks, drawing Crimpste's attention.

"We are on our way to Dapalos, to talk about the return of the Barazul," Crimpste replies.

"Oh well then, please tell him that a visit here once in a while would be good for morale," Zalot says, looking around at the plain faces around the room. Just as he finishes, two guards appear in the doorway, dragging a bloody figure behind them. They walk up to Zalot as they tighten their grasp on the prisoner's pale arms.

"We found this one in the valley to the northeast," the bigger of the two says, sliding the prisoner over.

The man, hiding his frame behind a shield of metallic skin, looks around the room as his brutish axe hangs close to the floor.

"Is that so, Onis?" Zalot asks, inspecting the prisoner as a trail of blood drips beneath his brow. Zalot walks over to the figure, placing his hand up against his chin and raises his face as he looks down into his beady green eyes. "These marauders just don't seem to want to leave us alone." He suddenly snaps the prisoner's head back, releasing his chin.

The group watches as the figure suddenly spits blood in Zalot's face as he chuckles. Struggling to break free from Onis and the other guard, he pauses as rage creases Zalot's face.

Zalot violently wipes the spit from his face, watching as the man smiles at the floor. "You and Wolf have my blessing to do what you want to this one."

Zalot turns to the two men as they face each other. The two quickly grab the man, turning around as they make their way outside. Their prisoner struggles to squirm away, but Wolf and his ally clench their fingers into his skin as they make their way out of the room.

Wolf, while not as intimidating as the other, is still a bulky man with armor made from pieces of debris from the battles he has fought in. His weapon of choice, a polearm nicknamed Dryden, drags against the stone. As the sound of the scraping echoes off the walls, they stop as the prisoner tries to jerk free.

"Let's play a game of 'you run' and 'we catch'," Wolf says, looking down into the green eyes sinking behind his pale eyelids. After a moment or two, a scream enters the barracks that sends Zalot into a giggle.

"What are these marauders you are talking about?" Crimpste asks.

"Just a rebellious outsider group that tries to start trouble," Zalot replies as he wipes the last bit of spit off his cheek.

"Should we be on our watch during our expedition?" Crimpste asks, causing Zalot to turn back to him.

"It's no worry, my men have complete control of it," Zalot replies as another scream echoes through the halls.

"Would you allow some travelers to stay in your Hold's inn?" Crimpste asks as his eyes catch sight of the night beginning to swallow up the daylight.

"Are you afraid of the monsters that hunt in the night?" Zalot asks, folding his arms.

Crimpste shakes his head, and turns back to the other mages as they continue to stand around in silence. "We are masters of the arcane and fear no manifestation of matter," Crimpste replies as the other mages nod their heads.

Zalot watches on with a smirk as the group begins to gather together in the entrance of the hall. "Understood, friend, but do be watchful of those nasty nocturnal creatures inside the canyon to the north."

The group turns to look out the doorway as the clouds above the growing mountains on both sides of the ridge snuff out the faint light given out by the twinkling stars. The ridge, massive in height, dwarfs the rest of the landscape, taking over as the darkness tries to make its way over its walls.

"I think we can handle any intrusions upon our journey," Crimpste replies, opening his hand to reveal a swirling fireball, which diminishes as he closes his hand.

Crimpste waves farewell to Zalot before walking out of the barracks. With a snap of his fingers, his horse leaps over the miniature fence and stops just shy of him. Following suit, the rest of the mages watch as their own horses do the same as they approach their owners. As the mages mount up, Zalot stands just outside the main hall alongside the other troops, watching as the last one mounts up.

"Ride safe," Zalot says as the group charges toward the edge of camp and the entrance to the ridge.

Once the darkness surrounds them, Crimpste stops the group, looking back at their darting eyes and emotionless faces. "Crusayder and Shlippmack, ride ahead with torches so we may travel with guidance.".

The two mages proceed to the front, each one pulling out a scroll from beneath their robes. They wave their hands over the scrolls, channeling the spell into their horses, which causes them to become beacons of light against the approaching darkness.

"Now, Canosan take Muertoz and do the same but this time at the back of the party," says Crimpster.

"Why do we have to get the back of the group?" Muertoz asks, pulling a scroll out from a bag hanging along the horse's side.

"I said so," Crimpste replies as Muertoz sneers before he and Canosan begin their trek to the back of the group.

They drop back with scrolls in hand as Crimpste turns back towards the guiding lights in the front. Lifting his hand, they begin forward onto the rocky terrain as the sound of their horses' steps echo off into the distance. The group continues to move along, listening to the screeching and gusts of air as it swirls around them. About halfway through the canyon, Crimpste looks back to see Minazue Hold shrinking down to a single speck before turning his head and noticing the bones of a massive creature alongside the road.

"Let us quickly move along, otherwise we might end up like that beast," Crimpste says, turning his attention forward as he watches the group stare at the remains.

Once the group passes by, their nerves begin to fray as the sounds of nearby beasts grow louder. Pushing forward, the group looks straight ahead at the exit as Dapalos remains just beyond the outskirts of the canyon. Exiting the canyon after a final turn to the left, their eyes catch sight of the skeletal frame of a house as a flickering light reflects off its pieces of metal. As the mages approach it with caution, suddenly a shadow flies across the wall in front of a broken post behind the light source.

As the group nears, they spot a roaring campfire, along with a shadowy figure standing inside the dusty room. Small in stature, the figure's shadow deceives all visitors by the drastic difference in its actual height. Just as they get within the circle of glowing light and out of the darkness, the figure spots the group with its long eyes, a smile revealing sharp teeth. To the mages' surprise, they find themselves face to face with a troll and all of its hairy and muscular skin peeking between sections of rags along its body.

"Are you alone, travelers?" the figure asks, sitting up against one of the makeshift walls.

Without a response, they cautiously ride closer as they keep their attention upon it, even as it sits quietly. The mages stop in their tracks when Crimpste dismounts from his horse, mere feet from the figure.

"Evening troll, we are merely a group of mages," Crimpste replies.

"Well then, may I ask you mages a question?" the troll asks before struggling to get back to its feet. Once back upon its silvery feet, the troll bounces across the room as it scrounges around for something.

"I am certain you may," Crimpste replies, brushing some of the dust from his robe.

"Did you happen to see anyone on your way through the canyon?" the troll asks, watching Crimpste sit down on a barrel next to the fireplace.

"We did not see anything through the darkness of the shadows," Crimpste replies.

"I knew he was too good of a worker," the troll mumbles before turning his attention to the flickering flames.

"May I ask your name?" Crimpste asks as the troll kicks one of the empty boxes into the fire, sending the flames toward the sky.

"My apologies. My name is Limzor," the troll replies, turning his attention as his eyes glow in the light of the fire.

"Greetings Limzor, I'm Master Crimpste and these are my fellow mages from the mage camp in Zalzona," Crimpste replies.

"Why are a group of mages traveling away from their camp?" Limzor asks as he looks back at the fire.

"That is a long story, which involves treachery and backlash," Crimpste replies as he watches Canosan walk out of the shadows of the growing flames.

"What about this worker you were talking about?" Canosan asks as Crimpste looks back at Limzor.

"He went inside that devilish feature and has yet to return," Limzor replies angrily.

"I can send two of my friends to search for your worker, if you would like," Crimpste says, causing Limzor to look over to him.

Limzor looks at Crimpste with a smirk as the other mages stare at one another, pointing as they try to figure out who he will choose. "I have nothing to offer you though, so your assistance would be for no fee."

"All we will require is food and some shelter for the night," Crimpste replies.

Limzor turns around quickly, and walks over to the bar shelf, opening a crate that was hiding behind it. From within the crate, Limzor pulls out a dusty bag with a lumpy bottom. "If you find him, you can have the bread that is inside." He then tosses the bag between Crimpste and the fire.

Crimpste nods his head as he points at Apocol and Crusayder. "You both can finish the mission the fastest."

Making their way outside, they watch as two bolts of lightning flare into the cloudy sky as they mount their horses.

"Where will we possibly find this worker?" Crusayder asks, looking down at Limzor.

"Over there," Limzor replies as he points toward a widening crevice alongside the rock wall of the canyon.

"We shall return shortly," Crusayder says, striking his horse as they take off out into the darkness of the night.

"I forgot to mention that the valley is rumored to be loaded with gryphon-like creatures," Limzor says, shifting his attention to Crimpste.

"That is of no importance, for my brothers are both strong in the arcane," Crimpste says as the two mages begin their trek toward the valley.

As the group watches on, the two mages quickly make their way to the entrance, their horses abruptly stopping. The two mages dismount as the horses stand motionless, looking at the entrance. Once inside the canyon, the mages gather themselves with a torch in one hand, holding a tight grip on their wands at the ready. Moving farther inside, the mages inspect the walls as feathers swirl around the air. Finding no trace of the worker, their blood runs cold as screeching echoes all around them. As they spin in circles, their feet stumble about the opening when they stop suddenly, catching sight of a line of nests upwards along the wall. Their eyes quickly focus in on the largest nest as they spot something within its branches. After taking a few steps closer, their torch light peels back the darkness, revealing the contents. Inside the nest was a body, as still as the eggs that sit on either side. The two mages then turn to each other before looking back to find a way upward.

"Have I ever told you how much I hate cliffs?" Crusayder asks, taking in the terrain around the nest.

"It will be easy. Just jump there and run the rest," Apocol says, lifting his torch closer to the ridgeline, revealing the path.

"WAIT! You aren't coming with me?" Crusayder asks, watching as Apocol silently steps farther away. Crusayder shakes his head as he approaches the wall before placing his hands upon a chunk of rock hanging over the edge. After struggling to pull himself up, Crusayder gingerly makes his way over to the nest as Apocol watches from below.

As he watches Crusayder approach the nest, Apocol spots shadows beginning to circle closer to Crusayder and the nest. "Hurry up and get him," Apocol mumbles, watching as Crusayder leans his body over the rim of the nest.

Just as Crusayder reaches his hands over, his feet give way, sending him crashing into the nest. Tumbling over the nest's contents, Crusayder's eyes drift upwards, seeing the shadows grow along the wall. Frozen among the broken branches, Crusayder watches as beasts fly downward, their sharp claws aiming for him. He quickly grabs the body and jumps over the rim just as the dagger-like claws rip holes in his cloak. Floating in the air, he reaches back and throws an open scroll toward the ground. Landing with a plume of dust, the hard ground softens, cushioning Crusayder's landing as his feet sink into the surface.

Once Crusayder is on solid ground, Apocol quickly turns his attention to the wall of darkness as beady red eyes pierce through. One by one, the figures step into the torch glow, revealing their true figures. A dangerous mixture of feathers and skin, the gryphons step forward, revealing their bird like faces, their wings crossed in front of their bodies. They spread their wings, showing their human-like arms and rows of feathers as their fingers bend back into formation. Before they can get any closer, Apocol aims his wand forward, snowflakes shooting from the tip. After mumbling incantations, solid links of ice shoot out from the wand and wrap around the gryphons.

"Will you hurry up, they won't be stuck all night," Apocol yells as the chains begin to lock as they break free from the wand.

Just as the ground returns to normal, Crusayder begins to run towards the entrance with the body over his shoulder.

Once the last bit of gryphon movement stops, Apocol rushes over to Crusayder to help take some of the dead weight off his shoulder. As they run, suddenly the gryphons extend their wings, shattering the chains into snowflakes. They turn their attention to the two mages continuing to make their way to the opening. Lifting off the ground, the two gryphons streak in their direction with their talons at the ready.

Just as the mages are about to reach the exit, Apocol stops, allowing Crusayder to get ahead as he turns back toward the gryphons.

Before the gryphons can get any closer, he throws down a frostbitten parchment which unravels as it slams into the ground. It absorbs the frosty texture and unleashes an icy blast, which drops the gryphons onto the sandy floor. While the gryphons are in a daze, Apocol quickly looks back, finding Crusayder standing safely outside the crevice. Just before Apocol begins to run out, he stops and turns back once more, watching as the gryphons struggle to shake their feathery heads.

Apocol stands as the gryphons lift off into the air above him as Crusayder looks on from the entrance. Suddenly, the gryphons drop from the air as their talons aim for Crusayder, who reaches inside his robe. Just as they get a wingtip away, Apocol pulls out his wand and slams it into the ground, creating an explosive blast of energy. The pulse sends the gryphons crashing into the rocky cliffs, allowing him time to run for the exit as Crusayder waits for him. Once he reaches the exit, he turns his head to see his horse alongside Crusayder as he mounts his own.

Apocol runs and grasps hold of the reins as they ride away quickly. Leaving the fallen ones in their dust, the two quickly watch as the camp's light grows from within the depths of the darkness. As they arrive to the group, Limzor rushes out of the doorframe, spotting the body on the back of Crusayder's mount. Crusayder lifts the body off and places it into Apocol's waiting arms. The two mages then lay the body up against a post as Limzor begins to try to shake the body, hoping to see the life return.

"Come on Zen, I know you're still there," Limzor screams as he continues to shake his shoulders. After a few moments of no response, suddenly his eyes open. In shock, Limzor steps back as Zen, with Muertoz's help, gets slowly back to his feet.

"I feel so weak and faint," Zen says, placing his fingers on the sides of his skull.

Crimpste quickly walks over, and hands Zen a scroll which glows as it touches his bones. The glow begins to surround him, and then fades away as the others look on.

Zen then rises from the post out of disbelief as he turns to Crimpste. "So you're a mage like me, I see."

"Well it's been a busy night, so we should all get some sleep," Limzor says.

The mages look around at each other, and then turn back at Limzor whose eyes wander.

"Our reward?" Apocol asks, turning Limzor's attention back to him.

"I guess you earned it," Limzor says as he pulls out some blankets in addition to the bread chunks. Handing a chunk of bread to each mage, Limzor waves good night before settling down next to the burning remains of the fire. He watches as the mages place their blankets on the old wooden floorboards before laying down upon them. Before the fire can turn to coal, the mages fall asleep as Limzor stands near the bar shelf with a bottle and some blank paper.

Chapter Six

A s the mages begin to wake, their eyes dart across the site, finding no trace of Limzor. However, looking over by the broken crates, the group finds Zen asleep with a bottle next to him. As the mages watch, Zen wakes, his eyes locking on the bottle and the contents within. Zen then breaks open the bottle and kneels before picking up the paper into his hands. After opening it, Zen looks down and slowly reads it to himself as the others look on in silence. Continuing to look on, they watch as Zen's mouth stops moving before taking a deep breath. They then watch as he places the paper to his side even as his eyes dart over to the group.

"Thank you, Limzor."

"What did it say?" Apocol asks, turning Zen's attention toward him.

"Limzor left him to allow him to join his mage brothers," Crimpste replies.

Apocol and the rest of the group nod their heads before they turn their attention to Zen as he stands up, using the crate as a brace. The group watches as he places the message inside his bag before stepping on a piece of the broken glass along the ground. Zen makes his way over to the group as they all step out from the broken doorway. The mages walk out of the building and mount up their horses, which await them next to a boulder sitting upon the sand. As they are about to take off, they stop and look down at Zen as he remains still in front of the doorway.

"Do you have a ride for the journey?" Crimpste asks.

Zen turns to a nearby farmhouse that sits in shambles, and watches as lightning explodes from the openings in the roof. Suddenly, the mages hear an enormous howl, which echoes over the land as an enormous wolf erupts from the back and charges toward the group. Its silvery fur shines against the sunlight, covering its entire body and face around forest green eyes. Before any of them can move, the wolf halts in front of Zen and squats downward. Allowing Zen to mount up, the wolf rises back up as Zen smirks over to Crimpste.

"Whoa, where did you get a wolf that size?" Canosan asks, trotting his horse over to Zen.

"Indigo here was passed down to me," Zen replies, petting Indigo's fur as he looks over at the horse.

"Very nice," Canosan replies as he looks down at his own horse in disappointment.

"Shall we go then?" Zen asks as he takes off ahead of the mages.

Crimpste shakes his head and takes off behind him as the others charge forward. As the charging mages approach the gigantic walls of stone that surround Dapalos, they slow down on their approach to the massive entrance. Before they can get any further, the group quickly turns off the road and stops at a makeshift stable just outside the city wall. Once their horses are secure, the group looks back at the sky-high walls in awe. The group begins to walk towards the city guards on both sides of the entrance, who turn towards them. The guards, heavily armored, carry their weapons carefully as their orange cloaks sway in the breeze.

"Welcome, Crimpste, to Dapalos," one of the guards says as they turn back to the hilly outskirts.

Just as they get inside, the mages look around as they admire the hustle of the city's center. To the right, they find various markets and carts servicing the citizens with various items. Meanwhile, in the center, was the Safekeeper, a stone building in the center with multiple floors, holding treasures from all over the land. Seeing the vast distractions, Crimpste turns back to the mages as they continue to admire the different things.

"Come brothers, Kolozi awaits us on top of that cliff," Crimpste says as he begins to walk over to the ramp.

As the mages walk towards the curving ramp, they continue to pass by different vendors selling chunks of food and hordes of weapons. Passing each one, the merchants stop themselves in mid-conversation and stare at the group. Making their way around the curve, the group finds themselves face-to-face with the massive castle. Pillars and towers erupt from the front walls. Many stories tall, the castle extends into the blue sky above, reaching from one end of the hill to the next. As the mages approach Kolozi's castle, they spot Limzor in the entrance, standing next to a gigantic figure.

Catching his attention, Limzor looks over to the approaching gang as they make their way into the shadows of the main castle. "Hope the fellows enjoyed the fresh bead!"

Before they can reply, Limzor waves farewell to the robed figure standing at his side. Limzor smirks as he turns around, just in time to see the mages making their way up from the bottom step. He quickly mounts up on his wagon before striking the horses in the front. As he takes off, the mages walk up the stairs and onto the front platform between two stone pillars. Climbing the final stair, they walk toward the doorway as a smirking figure catches Crimpste's attention.

"Greetings Kolozi," Crimpste says.

"Welcome Mages. I hear you've had a journey," Kolozi says.

Kolozi is an enormous figure under a silken robe. A pair of pointed shoulder pads on both sides, Kolozi's orcish skin covers up the shards of bones making up his neck. His forest-green skin covers his hands, which are covered in matching gloves which go up from his fingers. Revealing nothing else, his silvery mohawk drops to the side as his ears fold back. He watches as the mages group in front of him before they kneel in respect.

"Elder Kolozi, the Barazul enemy has struck our camp," Crimpste replies as Kolozi rubs his slight goatee.

"Come inside at once, for others have come forth bearing this same claim," Kolozi says as he starts to walk inside.

Crimpste leads the way as they proceed inside through the outer level of the castle. As they follow Kolozi into the throne room, they notice that throughout the outer part of the room were groups of the remaining classes. Separated by group, Kolozi had delegated the spell wielders to one side while the more physical sat all around. As they walk in, they stop in the middle of the room, just as all the loud talking turns to whispers. Kolozi walks over to his golden chair, covered in furs, and points the mages to a section of empty stools.

They quickly take their place while Muertoz pauses, looking around at the other groups. After casing the room, his eyes widen when he sees guards wearing Oriom Hill armor near a pillar on the other side. They were easy to spot, standing out from the rest with their leather chest piece and a square of orange-dyed fur.

As things are about to begin, Crimpste sits down in his place in front of the group before he looks over to a grayish skinned being in a dark purple robe. His orcish features are hidden behind a black witch's hat with a single glowing ruby in the center.

"Thanks for the scroll, Tharxion," Crimpste says, recognizing his friend.

"Glad to know it worked," Tharxion replies, lifting the brim to reveal his pale eyes.

Crimpste looks at Tharxion, and then turns to the other section to find a pair of eyes watching them. "Is that Yuskiocha?"

"It is," Tharxion replies, just as Kolozi stands up from his chair.

Kolozi looks around at the classes, who stop all their whispering to focus on him. "It appears we have an enemy that requires our united attention."

"We know, so what do you plan to do about this?" a voice erupts out mysteriously from behind the lines of one of the groups.

"See, each one of you have lost brothers from these troops," Kolozi replies as the other voices go mute. "Their kings or leaders have assembled an army to fight us into extinction."

"So where are they now?" Tharxion asks as the entire room looks at to him.

"They were last spotted forming an alliance inside their own castle," Kolozi replies, looking around the entire room

"What kind of alliance?" Crimpste asks.

"We are unsure," Kolozi replies as Crimpste turns back to the other mages behind him.   "This is why I have brought you here, so we can defeat them and end this decades-long battle once and for all," he continues.

There is a sudden giggle from out of one of the other sections, causing everyone to locate the source. From out of the front, a burly creature stands up as its mane plumes outward. Vines twist around his arm above his fur armor, making way to a stone mace with jewel shards pointing outwards. His blue eyes deliver a chilling stare back to Kolozi, above a face of sand-colored skin.

Narlugo is his name, and while one of the youngest shamans in the room, he has beaten titans all around the lands. Foreign to the mages, Narlugo looks down at his chair when suddenly sand erupts from the stones in the ground and forms a chair. "No shaman will ever work with any of you backstabbers."

As Narlugo sits back down, Yuskiocha rises, much to the chagrin of Stelton, the leader, and his pet timberwolf. Stelton is a tamer of beasts, both big and small, who comes from the lost islands that sit off the coast. His elvish features mesh with those of a human as his brownish color hides the scars along his frame. His armor is a mix of leathers and chains from his own blacksmith, surrounding him as his wooden bow sits alongside.

"You know, for a distant relative of mine, you sure lack the wisdom of who the enemy really is!" Yuskiocha yells.

"Be quiet! It's not my fault that mangy thing you call a wolf doesn't like you," Narlugo replies, watching as Yuskiocha looks down to the charcoal eyes of his pet.

"Excuse me?" Yuskiocha demands, turning to Narlugo as he and his wolf make their way forward. Before he can get any farther, Kolozi snaps, his face reddening under his green skin.

"I demand silence! don't you understand the seriousness of this threat!" Kolozi barks as Yuskiocha retreats to his seat.

Narlugo sits down on his chair with his arms crossed.

"We must show them the force that the Minazue is capable of," Kolozi continues. As the whispers begin again, Kolozi raises his hand, causing the whispers to fade into silence. "I can see you are skeptic about the possibility of working together, so I want the leaders to come down to the middle immediately."

One by one, the leaders look to one another as they make their way down, led by the mighty druid Nastale. Nastale, a druid by trade, comes from the camp located amongst the dense wilderness of the Kindred Moon. His skin is covered in patches of skin from the animals he had bonded with spiritually. Carrying fish scales along his arms, his hand grabs hold of the railing as he makes his way down to the main floor. Once beside Kolozi, Nastale turns his steer-like head toward the next leader making his way down.

Necromyr, the leader of the newest group amongst the clans, makes his way as he cracks the bones in his hands. His group is a diverse bunch of outcasts who made a camp to be free of any arcane intervention, so that they may use their own strengths to learn all they can. Wearing a black robe, he makes his way down as his bones crackle underneath his clothing. The rest of the leaders begin to form a circle around Kolozi, staring at each one as they arrive in the circle. As the rest watch with intent, Kolozi examines the leader's faces as they scowl from the discomfort.

"Look at yourselves, are you not tired of being divided over stupid questions of strength?" Kolozi asks, looking around the room at the leaders dropping their head.

The leaders stand silent with their heads down until suddenly a giant hand in a metal gauntlet rises from one of the sections causing Kolozi to look up. "I wish to unite, for I have lost brothers to this monster," Cappicola says.

Cappicola hides his body in thick plate armor yet stands tall as his brutish axe leans against his chair. His helm, shiny and new except for a single crack along one of the eyes, lifts off, causing the other warriors to turn their heads to him. One by one, the entire group begins to stand in unity, except for Yuskiocha and Narlugo, who continue to look around from their chairs. After a moment or two, Yuskiocha exhales before rising from his chair with a nod of his head, which causes Narlugo to do the same.

Kolozi looks back down at the leaders who are looking all around at the unification of their groups. "Our Minazue clan was once a united and strong tribe long ago."

The leaders begin to accept the idea, looking around at the other leaders as they stare upon their own groups.

"Let us unleash a roar to be heard through the land!" Kolozi yells.

After a pause, one by one, the leaders starting with Tharxion, lift their weapons into the air with a bellowing yell.

Kolozi smirks before raising his hand as a servant comes in, pushing a large crate into the center. The servant walks up and opens the crate, allowing Kolozi to reach in before pulling out different armors in various shades of black. Kolozi then throws some to each of the leaders to be given to their own groups. "These are to symbolize this mighty new beginning."

As they each put them on, they notice that on each armor a single large drop of red is stitched within each one.

"What is this symbol?" Yuskiocha asks, rubbing his finger over the symbol on his chest piece.

"This is to show that you are the new blood of the Minazue," Kolozi continues.

"Then our name shall be the BloodMinazue," Nastale says, causing the rest of the group to look about. Before long, each group nods their heads in approval of the name for this ragtag group.

Kolozi walks out from the center of the room and back towards his chair as the leaders' eyes follow him. As he gets to his seat, he glances over at the other Minazue council members, who are sitting to his side. "Now, by the names of Kolozi, Rozin, Lunasi, and Alarin you are now the mighty BloodMinazue."

As he finishes, the newly formed group raise their weapons up with a mighty roar, sending an echo down into the main town, causing the commoners in town to stop what they are doing. Lowering their weapons, the chamber door opens, allowing a group of Minazue inside. Each one packing their weapons to their side, helmets reveal nothing but their brownish eyes. The group consists of six Minazue, all bearing battle scars as they walk pass the guildies.

Out of wonder, Kolozi rises from his throne trying to find the cause of the commotion. "Who has entered this chamber without introduction?"

"Hunter Squad Five," a voice says just as the group steps through the crowd.

As his eyes meet the group, Kolozi scurries towards them in shock at the sight of their status. "What has happened?"

"We ran into a squad of Barazul soldiers," one of the troops in the front replies, carefully removing his metal helmet.

"Then I'm certainly glad you made it back Bachin and Del," Kolozi says, watching as another being steps forward next to the other.

"We do have other news," Bachin replies, looking around the room.

"Did everything go smoothly on the shores of Sopolm?" Kolozi asks.

"We were able to push them back, however many lives were lost," Del replies next to Bachin as he too begins to remove his helm, revealing his reddish hair trimmed tightly against his bluish scalp. They watch as the smirk disappears from Kolozi's face.

"Any other bad news?" Kolozi asks, placing his massive hands upon his face.

"We are sorry, sir, but we were forced to destroy the historic pier in order to hinder their intrusion," Bachin replies, looking over at the blood dripping from Del's face.

Kolozi's eyes widen as he sits back down and looks at the two in disbelief. "First they gain a new ally, and now they have taken our lone gateway to our allies in the north," Kolozi yells, slamming his fist into the throne.

"My lord, we did find out what they are planning next," Del says as he turns back to the group. They watch as one of the members walks forward and hands Kolozi a folded paper that he quickly opens.

As Kolozi finishes, his eyes widen as he looks back up at Del. "What is the name of the soldier that gathered this from the enemy?"

"Niko here was able to steal this from one of their generals," Del replies, looking over at Niko as he steps next to him.

Niko, the tiniest member of the bunch, is a troll like Limzor. Even with his tiny figure, Niko's body is covered in all black, in addition to a black bandana covering his mouth.

Kolozi stands up and turns toward the group. "They are heading back to ROA'MADI!" Kolozi yells, throwing the paper onto the ground. Out of the group, the leader Gunny steps out in front of the others.

A massive man wearing plated armor from his feet to his head, Gunny slams his foot forward into the ground, causing his giant sword to swing along his back. As the durability of his armor weakens from older battles, Gunny darts his black eyes all around the room. "What shall we do?"

"I want you to prove that you are the vicious slayer that your reputation has built you into," Kolozi replies.

Gunny then nods his head, and steps back into the group as Kolozi turns back to the Sopolm troops.

Kolozi then looks at Del and Bachin, who kneel before him. "Now, for you guys, I want you to enjoy the rest of the day, because come tomorrow you shall gather an army and head with Lunasi to the Spirit Sanctuary."

Del and Bachin nod and rise to their feet, walking through the BloodMinazue back into the main city as the guild turns their attention back to Kolozi.

"Excuse me sir, but what is the plan?" Mernerva asks as he steps in front of Nastale.

Mernerva, a high-ranking druid behind Nastale, stands tall with feathers all along his skin, his bird-like face twitching around the room. His tannish coloring blends with the room, allowing him to silently make his way forward.

"Well, we must take the fight to them and finish off the remnants of their tribes," Kolozi replies.

"Fighting them there might not be the best," says Mosenrath, sitting back against the wall as his feet cross. He sits back up before making his way into the shield of light, revealing his form. A massive staff sitting over his leathery armor, Mosenrath peels back his plain humanly skin to reveal the patchy furs like Nastale's skin. Lifting his hood off his head, the group watches as bull like horns appear on both side of his lion-like face.

"True, but we must take down the leaders in order for the rest to drop," Kolozi replies. As the guild begins to mumble amongst itself, Kolozi stands up and yells, "Enough with the questions! You shall rest tonight and then prepare for battle tomorrow."

"Wait, is the council not coming?" Mosenrath asks as Kolozi begins to scowl, clenching his teeth behind his green lips. Before Kolozi can say anything, Rozin the Domiala leader stands up from behind the table.

Rozin has been a council member for centuries alongside Kolozi. His frame is that of an average Domialan male, with pale skin that reveals nothing out of the ordinary behind his silken robe. The only bit showing his non-human side is the glowing that surges along his neck and face, which leads up to his constantly moving blond hair. The Domiala are nature loving people who have shared a bond with the rest of the Minazue to bring stability back to the world. Humanlike in their activities, the Domiala surround themselves with magical objects which help protect them from intruders. "They have enough power to not need us lagging behind. Now go and prepare yourselves."

Mosenrath turns back, feeling as some try to pull him farther from the council table. Arriving back into the group's depths, they kneel and scurry out of the chamber leaving the council alone.

Once out of the room, Rozin turns to Kolozi as he sits down on his throne once again. "No need to be angry. They are merely curious."

"True, besides, my anger shall be delivered to the head of the Barazul," Kolozi says. The others look on as he gets up from his throne and heads out of the chamber.

Rozin then turns to Alarin as he twists his silvery beard, taking in the vastness of the room. Realizing that Rozin was looking over at him, Alarin blinks his eyes, creating a reflective mirror in front of his face, revealing Rozin's stare.

"I have business at Oriom Hill so I will have to sit this out," Rozin says, reaching into the pocket of his robe. He pulls out a scroll, which explodes with light, allowing Rozin to teleport back.

Alarin looks around before getting up from his chair, brushing the wrinkles out of his robe. "Didn't even send us a farewell." Shaking his head, Alarin makes his way through the open doorway between the stone pillars.

Back outside, the guild walks around outside when they see Kolozi and Lunasi coming out of the castle.

Lunasi turns to Kolozi before turning back to look at the united group. "Mighty BloodMinazue, tomorrow you shall go forth and bring the heads of the dead back to Dapalos."

Afterwards, her rotting steed arrives behind two skeletal bodyguards, who stop in front of her. As chunks of flesh drip from off the beast, her eyes stare heavily into its open ribcage with a mixture of fondness and pity. As she places her feet along the bare ribs of the horse, she climbs into position as her cloak slips between the bones of the steed. She screeches as the horse rises upon its hind legs and then takes off in a dash.

"I have one favor to ask of you three," Kolozi mumbles as he looks over at Tharxion.

Before Tharxion can reply, Kolozi turns to Dockius and Nastale as they begin to follow behind Tharxion. The three guildies step forward and look to Kolozi as he waits for the three to gather towards him. Dockius, a mighty warrior, uses all the power that is holy as it chains throughout his metallic armor. His mighty sword gleams around his hand as Dockius places his helmet back over his pale face.

"How may we be of service to you?" Tharxion asks, speaking up from the group.

"Deep within Dapalos is a place known as Murmia's pit," Kolozi says. "Deep inside this pit is a creature known as Murmia Lominos, and I need you to defeat it for the citizens here."

The three begin to whisper amongst themselves as Kolozi watches on. "While we accept this favor, we have chosen Dockius to lead two of our strongest members inside," Nastale replies.

"Oh, and who does he have in mind for this venture?" Kolozi asks as he turns his attention to Dockius.

"Well, Sire, I have chosen Bulling and Grugnor," Dockius replies as he points out the two men from the group.

"Very well, now while the rest ride through the city you three shall follow me to the pit's entrance," Kolozi says.

The four then walk off towards a crevice hidden behind the solid rock while the rest of the group spreads out. Once through the crevice, the group makes their way down a ramp into a foggy section of the city with Kolozi at the lead. They walk down towards the end of it as it gives way to a massive opening surrounded by various stone formations. As the guildies are looking into the cave, two beings appear from out of the fog into the beams of sunlight.

"Glad to see you alive Fogadorn and Molozel!" Kolozi yells as they stop just shy of the group.

"Greetings, Sire, the way to Murmia has been all cleared out as you requested," Fogadorn says, wiping the sweat and ash from his bluish forehead.

"Oh yeah, those mobs never saw us coming," Molozel replies as he places his smoking launcher back on his back.

Just before the group members can lose focus, Kolozi quickly turns around and gathers their attention. "These two mercenaries have taken out everything ahead of the leader."

"That should make it quicker for us," Bulling says as he looks down at his tiger companion.

"Watch out, that demon is no easy feat," Fogadorn says as he and Molozel step to the side, allowing the group to pass.

"Thank you, and here's the payment I promised you," Kolozi says as he hands over a parchment sack.

The two men then nod their heads and walk out of the valley to get back into the city. The three then begin to approach the cave with caution as their minds race about what is waiting for them inside. Just as they are about to step inside, they quickly look back at Kolozi as he stands alone in the thinning fog.

"Good luck, and don't worry. If anything gives you trouble, I have something for them," Kolozi says as he points to the boulders in the air above their heads. The group then turns back around, stepping forward as they stare deeply into the darkness of the cave.

Chapter Seven

O nce inside, the group finds themselves walking deeper into an abandoned mine with an orange glow from the lava flowing throughout. Looking around, they find ash covering every surface as a burning smell twists into their nostrils. The three turn to look at each other, when suddenly a gigantic roar causes the ash to rain down from the rocks above them.

Bulling quickly pulls out his crossbow from underneath his silken cloak. Bringing it forward, he turns as the others pull out their swords as they begin to walk through the falling dust. Their eyes darting around, the group continues deeper into the cave, listening to the echoes as they bounce off the walls. After walking for a few moments, they come to an opening in the mine where the noise becomes louder. The group looks ahead as they see the main chamber, which is a combination of platforms and old mining carts. On the middle platform stands a gigantic figure, wielding a glowing blade with a bone hilt, as two sorcerers in dark robes kneel at its feet. The being, towering over everyone, stands between the platforms and the swirling lava beneath it. Its skin is a mixture of bone and shreds of metal, covering all of him except for demonic eyes above his fanged mouth. As a burnt metal helmet sinks below his cheeks, the figure keeps his gaze upon the trembling sorcerers as their magic channels through the platform.

His eyes widening, Dockius turns to the others as they continue to look on in awe. "If that's Murmia, then we might just have ourselves a challenge."

"I don't know … I've seen bigger," Grugnor replies as he readies his daggers.

"Well then, let's do this thing," Bulling says as he begins to reach his arm behind his back, pulling out some bolts from their quiver.

The three walk forward when suddenly they notice that, between them and Murmia, stands two darkly dressed figures with hoods covering their faces. Beside them, their shadows lift from the ground and solidify next to them. In addition, trying to hide in the shadows was a demon whose red eyes are barely visible through the darkness. Grugnor and Dockius turn to Bulling, whose hands struggle to place a bolt into the chamber of the crossbow.

"Try not to kill all of them at once," Grugnor says as he watches Bulling look down as the bolt clicks into place.

"I'll try and save some for you," Bulling replies before snapping off the first bolt.

The shot zips through the air, hitting the shadowy creations, followed by the mage directly behind it. Watching on, the hooded enemy cries as it falls from the platform as the shadow dissolves into the ash surrounding them. The second figure and its minion sharply turn towards the three, manifesting a sword of darkness before rushing for an attack. As the two are approaching, Bulling stands strong next to Dockius as both draw their swords in defense. Just as the attackers are about to reach them, they both suddenly stop in their tracks. They suddenly see a pair of all white eyes widen from behind the darkness of its hood and its feet give way. Crashing into the stone ground, the plume of ash reveals Grugnor with a dagger to his side as black blood drips to the ground.

The shadowy demon struggles to break free from fear-induced paralysis, watching as his ally fades from this realm. It then turns its attention back to the group as its anger intensifies. The demon begins to tense up as it breaks loose and continues its charge. Before the demon can get any closer, Bulling's lion jumps off another platform, pouncing on the demon and dragging it into the shadows. Once the moaning silences, the lion reappears with its sharp teeth around the neck of the demon.

Dockius then drags the two corpses and throws them into the

lava as Grugnor takes a piece of cloth out to wipe the blood from his dagger. As they turn around, Dockius suddenly crashes into the wall as the others look on. Just before he slides to the ground, they watch as his armor shines through the darkness, a single crack penetrating the durable metal. Bulling and Grugnor then quickly turn around to see Murmia behind them, raising his sword to strike once again. Unleashing another screaming swing, they manage to dodge it as they run towards Dockius, who leans against the wall.

"Hey, are you in one piece?" Bulling asks as he slides to Dockius's side.

"Yeah, just distract him. I want payback," Dockius replies as he pushes himself off the rocky wall. Before they can reply, Dockius charges forward jumping onto another platform.

"How does he want us to do that?" Bulling asks as he turns to watch Grugnor disappear just before the sword can make its way around.

Continuing to watch, Bulling's eyes shift to a satchel sunk beneath his cape. He opens it up, revealing a glass sphere, a raging inferno erupting within. As Murmia turns his attention to Grugnor, Bulling runs up and buries it within the levels of ash in Murmia's way. After covering up the orb with the surrounding ash, Bulling hides behind a boulder that Dockius had broken free and watches as Grugnor leads Murmia in its direction. At the last possible moment, Grugnor bolts for the rock where Bulling is hiding, dodging the pile to avoid revealing the trap. As he gets to Bulling, Grugnor turns as they watch as Murmia steps onto the orb, jets of flames firing in all directions. They watch as the floor around Murmia becomes a bed of flames as it causes him to tumble to the ground, sending a shockwave through the chamber.

"Take this!" Dockius yells from the shadows.

They watch as he jumps from the cliffs with his sword gleaming with magic. Dockius lands as his sword pierces Murmia's rib cage, allowing the soul fragments inside to escape. As the breath leaves Murmia's body, Dockius rises back to his feet. Once the dust settles, the two watch as Dockius climbs the rib fragments around the grayish muscles, pulling his sword out from the torn cavity.

"Hey, while you're there, don't forget the token of victory,"

Grugnor says, pointing his finger toward Murmia's corpse.

Dockius looks and kneels over the spreading crevice as the muscles relax. His eyes widen as he reaches down, lifting out the heart, which beats faintly still in his hand. He turns to Bulling. "Hey Bulling, wrap this up for me."

Bulling walks over to him as he pulls out a glowing bag from within one of the many hanging from around his belt. He opens it as a vortex of air sucks in all the ash nearby, watching Dockius drop the heart inside. Once inside, Bulling closes the bag up, the chaos of wind fading as he ties it up. As they walk back over to Grugnor, green fluid begins to drip from the bottom. Together, the three dust themselves off before making their way over to the entrance of the cave. Making their way through the fiery environment, Bulling stops and turns his head over to the cliff side. His eyes watch as shadows dart across the orangish glow. Dockius and Grugnor then stop ahead of him, looking up in shock as their eyes meet those of angry demonic creatures with eyes glowing red.

"Let's get out of here!" Bulling yells as he begins to run towards the entrance.

Dockius and Grugnor take off after him, watching as the beasts begin to jump down and chase after them. Out of breath and afraid their legs will give out just shy of the entrance, they muster up enough energy to run outside, just as massive boulders crash on top of the creatures. Looking back, the group brushes themselves off as their eyes wait for any trace of movement. Seeing none, they turn towards Kolozi as Bulling pulls out the bag, which continues to drip on the floor.

"What is that?" Kolozi asks, looking at the green stain welling up from the bottom of the bag.

"The heart of Murmia," Bulling replies, extending the bag's opening to reveal the depths of its inventory. He then reaches in and lifts the still heart to Kolozi's surprise.

"That's the heart of the beast?" Kolozi asks, cautiously taking a step forward.

"Indeed Sire, but the path wasn't as clear as you were told," Grugnor says as Bulling places the heart over the bag as the vortex of air charges upward. They watch as the heart sinks down within the seams of the bag as it settles down in size.

Kolozi shakes his head before looking up at the level above, where he finds Molozel trying to hide in the shadows of the cave-like roof.

Molozel gulps as his sight locks onto Kolozi, and he turns to Fogadorn who suddenly takes off toward the city.

"I'm out of here!" Molozel yells as he takes off after Fogadorn as both charge out into the city streets.

"My apologies, I was misinformed," Kolozi replies angrily as he clenches his giant hand.

"It is quite alright. We thoroughly enjoyed the challenge," Dock-ius says, looking down at his sword, seeing the faint stain of blood.

Kolozi smirks, and then begins to walk toward Bulling, who turns his palm upward as the bag sits on top of it. Kolozi grabs it and opens it to see the heart floating through the open space inside. Kolozi then closes the bag back up, and walks away from the group as they look on in silence. As he heads up the stairs, he stops mid-way before turning his attention back to them. "The people of Dapalos are forever in your debt."

The group bows as they head through an opening along the side of the wall, finding the day to be over as only stars sit above them. As they look around, they find the streets empty, as most of the commoners have returned to their homes, leaving nothing but the city lights. They make their way through the barren roads into the heart of the square, where heavily armored guards ride past them toward Kolozi's castle. Arriving at center of the city, two guards hang behind the others as they appear in front of them, dragging a limp body.

"I never knew Troxin was a traitor," one of the guards says, turning to the other. As the guards continue past them, the group make their way towards one of the larger stone buildings along the street.

Grugnor reaches for the handle, surprised when it suddenly swings open as Molozel and Fogadorn come storming out. Trying to escape with their armor slinking loosely, two guards follow in their footsteps as they head towards the archway leading to the exit. The group turns their attention back to the inn as they continue inside. Once inside, the man behind the counter places a drink in front of one of the patrons before turning to the group. His eyes widen behind the shadows of the faintly lit room when he notices the symbol on their armor.

"You're with the BloodMinazue? You must want to join the others in the tavern room," the man says.

Unsure, the three follow him through a side doorway where they find two other members sitting at the bar in a slightly quieter atmosphere. The three step forward, which causes the wolf laying around the stool to lift its grayish head from its paws.

As it glares upon the group, Stelton glances at them briefly before turning back to his half empty mug. Reaching his skeletal hand around the handle, Stelton lifts it upwards to his curling pale lip. After gulping down some of the liquid, Stelton lowers it back down to the counter. "Well, I see you three are still alive."

"Yeah, that thing had no chance," Bulling says, taking a seat beside Stelton.

"Let me introduce myself. My name is Stelton and this foul thing is Grummore," Stelton replies, pointing over at Grummore on a stool beside him.

Grummore slams down his glass, rattling the wooden shelf as he turns his head, his leathery armor shifting with his movement. "I'm not foul, I'm a slayer."

"Whatever you say," Stelton chuckles, trying to avoid Grummore's angry stare.

"Anyways, the others had enough excitement and called it a night," Grummore replies.

"So, what was the deal with those guys running out of here?" Grugnor asks, sitting down next to Grummore as the bartender places a drink down in front of him.

"No idea, but we heard that Kolozi wanted to see them," Stelton says, looking around at the others nodding their heads.

Returning to their drinks, the group begins to settle down when suddenly a glass shatters behind them, causing them to whip around. Finding shards of glass spread around a wooden table, they look up to find an orc with glassy eyes staring at the large sword next to him. After a few moments, they watch as the orc sneers and he shifts his sight over to them. The massive orc slams his fists into the shards of glass and pushes himself up to his feet. His uneven teeth protrude from his upper lip as his eyes redden with rage as he turns his head to look at each of them. "You got a problem?"

"No, but it appears that you do," Stelton replies as he looks down at the broken glass hanging from out of it greenish skin.

"You think you're so tough, but I would have killed Murmia if Kolozi would have just asked," the orc grumbles as his chest tightens, showing his muscles pulsing beneath his skin.

"You are just a drunk orc," Stelton answers with a grin. He then turns back to his drink as the others follow suit, while the other patrons remain silent. Unbeknownst to them, he angrily stumbles around the table before nudging his massive shoulders into Dockius, causing him to spill his drink all over the counter and onto the stone floor below.

"Who in the hell do you think you are?" Dockius asks as he jumps off his chair, turning as he stares over at the orc as he braces against one of the stools.

The orc takes a step back and starts to laugh as Dockius brushes the drops from his armor. "I'm this city's blacksmith and I'm tougher drunk than you are any day." The group watches as the orc struggles to flex his arms.

Dockius shakes his head as he turns back around, when suddenly something squeezes his shoulder, causing him to look back. He turns back to find the blacksmith with his enormous hand around his shoulder.

"I demand a fight with any of you BloodMinazue fools as a show of strength," the blacksmith roars, pushing Dockius into the side of the counter.

"I'll take that fight," a voice replies, causing the patrons whispers to fall silent.

The blacksmith turns around to find Cappicola standing in the doorway with his sword in hand. The blacksmith stumbles over to his table, grabbing his sword as it lays flat against the wooden top. Once his hand was around the grip, the blacksmith makes his way over to the doorway with little regard for those around him. Stepping out into the faintly lit street, the blacksmith places his giant sword in front of him as he turns to Cappicola. "Okay, tough guy, bring it on."

"I'd have it no other way," Cappicola replies, lowering the front of his helmet as he readies his sword into position.

As the blacksmith charges wildly at Cappicola, Grummore appears in the doorway to watch the commotion unfold. Standing against the doorway off to the side, Grummore watches as the blacksmith attempts an attack, only to watch it fall harmlessly. "Don't kill him Cappi, we don't need any bloodshed."

Cappicola turns back to the blacksmith as he swings wildly, shoving the orc into a pile of barrels. Cappicola shakes his head as watches as the blacksmith knocks over two of them, drunkenly attempting to get into position. He watches once again as the blacksmith charges hysterically. Then, before the blacksmith can strike him, he moves out of the way tripping the drunken blacksmith. The blacksmith falls to the ground, causing his sword to slide into some crates in the alley nearby.

"This fight is over." Cappicola walks back into the inn out of pity, allowing the blacksmith to stumble to a knee.

"That's the best you got," the blacksmith gurgles as he hiccups in a drunken stupor. Cappicola pauses in the doorway to consider his words before continuing inside, further angering the blacksmith orc.

The blacksmith knocks over one of the pile of crates and screams out, "You coward!"

Quickly, Cappicola stops and turns around to face the blacksmith as he continues to struggle to get to his feet. Overcome with rage, Cappicola runs up, and swings his sword, striking the blacksmith with the flat part of the blade across the side of his head. The blacksmith's face crashes to the ground as Cappicola turns around, placing his sword back into its scabbard. He remains motionless in the street, and the patrons return to their seats as Cappicola sits down where the blacksmith had been seated. As they settle back down to drinks, the barkeeper watches as two guards come by and lift the blacksmith before taking him out of sight of those inside.

"I was just coming to see if you guys had seen them," Cappicola says as he looks over at the group.

"Were you actually worried about us?" Grugnor asks mockingly before lifting his drink to take a sip.

"Not really. Just didn't feel like telling Tharxion you guys are not coming back," Cappicola replies as he takes a gulp from the blacksmith's drink.

The group then shares a laugh before they quickly finish their drinks and get up from their chairs. As they are walking toward the door, Cappicola drops off his empty mug at the innkeeper who simply waves farewell. Making their way through the bar, the group steps outside into the approaching darkness. They walk through the empty town square towards a stone building of equal height just blocks away. This building was quite different, not just in material but that, hanging from the top wooden posts, was a massive banner containing the sigil of the newly formed BloodMinazue.

When they arrive at the building, Cappicola walks ahead of them and opens the door, allowing the others inside. Once through the panels of wood, the group looks around at their sleeping friends, struggling to make due with every open space. As they try to find a single opening, they manage to dodge the sleeping members, their eyes catching sight of a pair of open hammocks. Arriving at their location, they place their weapons down beneath the hammocks and lay down, shutting their eyes. After a moment or two, the silence is broken by a sniffling cough.

"Holy Domiala, what is that smell?" the voice asks.

"Excuse me, Amadeas, but the Domiala's smell is loveable," another voice replies, echoing from the other side of the room.

"Nice try, Mosen, but that was an epic fail," Yuskiocha cuts in.

"The name is Mosenrath," Mosenrath replies as Yuskiocha shakes his head in the darkness.

"Will you guys shut up? Some of us are actually trying to sleep," another much deeper voice replies.

"You tell them, Visuvium," Nastale replies as he stretches in his hammock. After a low chuckle spreads, the talking gives way to silence as the group settles down before falling back to sleep.

Chapter Eight

The next day arrives with the group waking up to the same bustling commotion as they saw the previous day. Once the group gets out of the building, they begin to watch as a mixture of different classes run around the city. Then, through the crowd, two of their members come walking towards them from the direction of a large building across the road.

"Hey Torem and Methyl, when did you get up?" Narlugo asks, stretching out his arms, nearly striking Yuskiocha and Tharxion nearby.

"Been up for a while," Methyl replies. Even as he tries to hide behind oversized armor, Methyl approaches the group with his red mohawk leaning over the side. Matching only the insignia on his shirt, Methyl's skin was the same color as the bones of the skeletal zombies that hide in the darkness.

"Yeah, sorry, just wanted to see if I got Navarra's letter," Torem adds before spitting saliva onto the floor just shy of his metal boots. Torem is a large statue of a man whose tan skin stands on par with the cuffs of the links in his armor. His axe hanging to the side, Torem looks around at the wandering bunch in front of him.

"Oh, so how is she joining us in this fight?" Tabias asks, turning Torem's attention to him.

"She says that she will meet us on the border between the lands," Methyl replies, causing Torem to shift his attention back.

Tabias nods as the group quickly gathers up when the crowd suddenly clears a path, revealing two guards stepping aside for Kolozi's arrival. As Kolozi comes closer, the entire group kneels in front of him and his two guards.

"Greetings BloodMinazue, I will be accompanying you to the border of Volzia, as a show of trust to the those who remain on the fence," Kolozi says. They nod their heads as Kolozi looks over in the direction of Cappicola. "By the way Cappicola, our blacksmith sends his apologies."

"I'm just sorry it came to a fight, but I care to see no Minazue blood shed by our own hands," Cappicola says, relaxing his head to allow his eyes to catch sight of him.

"Understood, ok well there is one last order of business," Kolozi says as he turns back to see two guards escorting Molozel and Fogadorn over.

"We are sorry Lord Kolozi, we didn't know those things return if you just simply leave their bodies," Fogadorn whimpers before wiping a line of tears off his cheek.

"That is no excuse, and if it wasn't that Bachin needs more troops for his fight I would have you in exile!" Kolozi yells before calming himself down. The group watches as two guards push them over to Bachin and Deliver, who are waiting by the entrance. Kolozi watches them leave through the exit, then turns around back to the group.

"What is they're punishment?" Bulling asks, feeding a chunk of meat to his lion sprawling out on the dirt.

"To help defend from another attack by our enemies abroad," Kolozi replies. As Kolozi is about to continue, a city guard suddenly steps out from the doorway causing the group to split in half.

"Sorry to interrupt you Lord Kolozi, but the Imperial Dragos scroll you requested is awaiting you," the guard says before stepping to the side to open the pathway.

"Thank you, Aloruan," Kolozi replies as Aloruan bows before walking back inside the darkness of the tower.

"Whoa, did he say the Imperial Dragos scroll?" Mosenrath asks, his mind wandering at the thoughts of the power of an Imperial Dragos.

"You didn't expect us to walk there did you," Kolozi replies with a smile.

"I thought those scrolls were only myths made up to keep outsiders from abandoning their home cities," Lukain says as the others smirk at her. Lukain, with a mixture of human and elven traits, carries around her flowing brown hair to her side to prevent enemies from getting the drop on her. Protruding from her back was a second set of defense thorns that appeared after she morphed with one of the local beasts from her land.

"Those mythical beasts of the scroll await us at the top," Kolozi says, beginning to make his way through the group and into the doorway.

The group watches as he disappears into the shining light tunneling through a hole in the roof. They quickly climb up the stairs before making it to the roof where Kolozi and Aloruan stand in silence. That's when their eyes catch sight of the massive beast and its wings that hang over the side. Its amber scales run from nose to tail as metal plating attaches to every inch as additional protection. A line of thorns goes from between its eyes all the way toward the tip of its tail. These were broken up by imperial draper, which sits just under Kolozi hand.

Kolozi then mounts up on the creature as the group continues to look on in disbelief. They watch as he waves farewell as the dragon flies off, avoiding the buildings as it leaves the others in a gust. Once Kolozi disappears from the city limits, the group turns their attention back to Aloruan who smiles, revealing his hidden tusks.

"So has anyone flown one of those before?" Aloruan asks, his eyes moving from left to right waiting for an answer.

They look at each other with a slight hesitance as they turn back to him in silence.

Aloruan smirks as he reaches inside his dragon scale robe and pulls out a golden scroll. He rips open the scroll with his tusks, causing the scroll to unleash a vortex into the air above the tower. Suddenly, a dragon's head peeks out of the vortex and then disappears before its body explodes from out of the swirling air. The dragon lands with a tremendous shock in front of one of the members, paralyzing him in disbelief.

"Tyrodris, you are first," Nastale replies, looking over at the trembling human standing in the dragon's shadow.

Struggling to regain his wits, Tyrodris struggles to move his limbs as the dragon sneers out a bit of smoke. Catching his breath, he approaches the creature before placing his hand on the scaly exterior of the beast. Tyrodris cautiously gets on, surprised when it suddenly takes off from the pavilion before he can take another breath. One by one, the others mount up as more dragons appear from out of the fading vortex above and watch as they quickly speed away from the edge of the city. Once the last dragon lowers its wings on the platform, the last member pauses briefly at the side of the creature.

"Come on up, Oxala," Aloruan says, pointing toward the top of the creature.

Oxala the final member is an orc by birth, except it was difficult to tell by the various chunks of other animalistic features that make up his frame. He takes a deep breath and gets on before quickly grabbing hold of the reins as it takes off. As Aloruan watches on, the dragon quickly storms out of the city toward the blazing sun, sinking beneath a layer of clouds. Once the group unites behind him, Kolozi begins to fly towards Miralande, a camp which harbors the Minazue troops before battle.

Watching as Kolozi is flying over the land, Nastale turns to Tharxion with a look of confusion on his face. "Aren't we going to Roa'madi?" Nastale asks, drawing Tharxion's gaze toward him.

"Right after we make a quick morale stop," Tharxion replies as Nastale nods before turning his attention back to the vast lands beneath.

As the group follows behind Kolozi, a plume of gray smoke catches their attention from the distance. Kolozi's eyes widen as he slams the leathery straps against the dragon's scales, causing it to boost its speed. Struggling to keep up, the others do the same as smoldering ruins reveal themselves over the hillside. The group looks down at the fragments of the once prosperous city, finding it stuck inside a mist of resentment as well as confusion.

As Kolozi and the group are descending, the ruins struggle to keep shape, the bodies of the town's citizens laying all about. Swooping downward, the dragons land on top of a vast platform, which cracks beneath their combined weight. Once the final dragon secures itself, the group watches as some of the wounded charge up from the darkness. Making their way forward, they watch as they dismount from their dragons led by Kolozi. Stepping away, the dragons unleash a stream of flames into the air just below the clouds. The streams unite and swirl around until suddenly a portal appears from within the blazing inferno.

As it opens to full capacity, the dragons lift off the platform and fly into the circle. Disappearing into the vortex, the group turns their attention toward the town as they inspect the ruins, except for Kolozi who turns to the struggling soldier leading the troop.

"Tell me what happened here, who has done this?" Kolozi demands, grabbing the soldier's fragile armor and lifting him up.

"Put him down, I can tell you that," a familiar voice says.

"Alarin," Kolozi replies, dropping the soldier as he turns around to see his fellow council member.

"They came in waves and destroyed the camp with precision," Alarin says, watching as the soldiers struggle to drag themselves together.

"Are you telling me that the Barazul is behind this?" Kolozi replies, looking at the destruction.

"Indeed, and so far, we have counted 15 lives lost," Alarin says.

As the two walk away into the ruins towards a building, the group spreads around to get a better look. Just as Oxala and another member begin to walk past an area of stones, a groan stops them in their tracks. Looking over, they find no trace of life, just the destruction of the forge where travelers could go to create weapons from the resources around the town. Before they can turn away, another dying groan causes them to run over, attracting those nearby to follow them to it. When they arrive, their eyes widen as they find a guard severely hurt as blood gathers on the ground around him.

Oxala kneels, removing the guard's hand to reveal the jagged edges of the open wound. He then pulls out a vial containing a swirling liquid, opening it above the wound as a green mist covers it completely. Screaming in agony, the guard calms as he looks down at the wound, which is beginning to heal. The guard then struggles to get back to his feet.

"Is everything good?" Canosan asks, arriving to the group

"He saved my life," the guard replies before taking another look at the new area of skin.

"So, what happened here?" Madagno asks, pulling his robe back as he kneels at the edge of the dissipating pool of blood.

The guard sits down on the edge of the flipped cauldron as his mind races. "Well, it was a normal day and then something screamed from behind one of the buildings."

Before the guard can speak another word, a hooded figure appears from the shadows and jams his dagger through his back. As the guard falls into the grass with the knife hanging outside, the figure begins to run away from the group and toward the open exit.

"Guards, it's one of them!" Oxala yells as he and Madagno give chase after it.

The others turn around and watch as the figure's hood drops as he runs past them, revealing its Barazul traits. Before he can reach the exit, he suddenly stops as the earth beneath him begins to tremble and quake. He then looks down as large vines erupt from within in the crevices and knot themselves around his legs. Watching him struggle to break free, the group begins to gather as they place themselves between him and the exit.

Kolozi and Alarin walk out, catching a glimpse of the intruder trying to free himself. Just as the two leaders begin to walk over, the vines loosen, allowing the intruder to kick them away. However, before taking another step, he watches as Mosenrath throws a scroll from his bag, which releases a magical gust that sends the intruder crashing into the rocky street. As the air releases from his lungs, they watch it lay motionless along the stones. With the intruder unconscious, the two leaders walk up as they try to decide what to do next.

"Gunny, I want you and Mosenrath to take this intruder up to that post and do whatever you have to in order to find out information," Kolozi says as he points to a ramp leading up into a command post for the guards of the town.

Thoranbluff and Rakagar then walk towards the body, each grabbing hold of an end before lifting it into the air. The two make their way to the top as Mosenrath and Gunny follow behind them. One of the most renowned brutes in the land, Gunny wears the black ash armor that he created. Meanwhile to his side, his enormous sword swings across his back. As they are about to get to the top, the intruder awakens and begins to squirm free until Mosenrath strikes him again with his wooden staff. Thoranbluff and Rakagar then lay him down upon a flat piece of wood on top of two boulders. They then make their way down the stairs, standing among the others to watch the action from the bottom.

Gunny turns to Mosenrath with a smirk as he grabs the figure by the neck, and roars in its face. Rattled, the figure twitches his eyes around the space before shaking his head as he turns to them with a grin, blood dripping from his lip. Gunny, out of anger raises him off his feet, watching as his shaking hands reach for his hand. Watching as the intruder struggles to catch a breath, Gunny looks down at the crowd beneath him. "Why did you do this, and why are you here?"

The Barazul looks at the two with a chuckle as he feels Gunny's grip loosen, and then spits in Gunny's face.

Mosenrath looks at Gunny, eyes widening in shock as the Barazul tries to peel back some of Gunny's fingers. Before it can make any progress, Gunny's hand tightens, causing him to squirm once more.

"Now you asked for it," Mosenrath says, watching as the color fades from the Barazul's face.

Gunny turns to the edge of the tower, hanging the Barazul beyond the platform.

Watching as his feet sway in the air, Kolozi looks from below as the two stand along the platform, shaking their heads. "Gunny, just drop him and get it over with."

Gunny and Mosenrath turn to one another as the group roars, causing the platform to shake. Mosenrath then watches as Gunny pulls the intruder back inside, placing himself between him and the edge. Gunny turns back to Mosenrath who begins to nod his head causing Gunny to look back at the fearful intruder.

"Have a nice trip," Mosenrath says, watching as him continues to try to get free.

Gunny smiles when suddenly he tosses the intruder off the edge with one of his massive arms, causing the Barazul to fall toward the remnants of a canopy. The intruder then falls through, crashing to the floor, causing debris to crumble on top of him. As Mosenrath and Gunny stand on the tower, Kolozi turns to Judication and Tharxion who are watching alongside him.

"You two check, and make sure he's dead," Kolozi says.

The two robed figures walk towards the building, squeezing their way inside. As they watch the hanging fronds, Judication points as he spots the body underneath a toppled roof column. Arriving at the body, they kneel when they catch sight of the slight movement of his chest.

"Wow all that show, and this guy is still alive," Judication says, looking over at Tharxion.

"Yeah well, we're here to make sure he's dead," Tharxion replies as a shard of a purple crystal lifts from his wrist.

"Let's just get this over with," Judication says.

"Sounds good, let me just put this beast out of its misery," Tharxion replies as he looks down at the faintly conscious body. Tharxion then stabs the shard into the center of his chest just as the shard begins to glow. Watching as the life fades from the body, Tharxion lifts the shard out and watches as the fluctuating glow stabilizes. Tharxion then puts the shard inside a tiny black pouch and walks back over to Judication. "Let's get out of here."

As they step from out of the rubble, they find Kolozi standing in front of the others, waiting for them. "Was he dead?" Kolozi asks, watching as they approach with no sign of the intruder.

"Sorry Gunny, your strength is not what it used to be, but don't worry I took care of it," Tharxion says, revealing the bright crystal shard.

Gunny shakes his head in disbelief as Mosenrath makes his way down from the ramp. As they make their way toward Kolozi, Tharxion and Judication walk away from the broken shambles and towards the others. As the group gathers, Kolozi turns around and looks at them as they gather in the shadows of the tower.

"I have received notice that the Barazul are now heading to their main town in the Requinos Glade," Kolozi says, shocking everyone.

"Why are they going to the Requinos Glade?" Grummore asks, placing a book back inside his robe.

"They're going there in search of recruits, and rumor has it they have arrived at their stronghold already," Kolozi replies.

"We must destroy the fiends who have brought harm to our people," Nastale says, receiving a roaring reply.

"You all are truly a guild of brothers," Kolozi replies.

"We, the BloodMinazue, shall take the fight to them," Gunny roars, lifting his sword high into the air.

"Indeed, you must, however I must leave you and fly back to Dapalos," Kolozi replies. A bit in shock, the guild watches on as Kolozi turns as his imperial dragos steps silently towards him. Kolozi then mounts up, waving farewell before the dragon flaps its wings to take off. They watch as Kolozi takes off towards Dapalos and into the glare of the sun.

As the guild watches Kolozi fade in the distance, Tharxion step forward and turns to the group. "Brothers, we are not cowards like the Barazul and we shall destroy them," he roars, lifting his wand into the air. The members unite in a roar as all the class leaders step forward, walking up next to Tharxion.

"We shall destroy them for all our Minazue brothers," Gunny says, raising his sword into the sky.

Once again, the guild roars aloud, but as they are doing so a howl shakes the camp. The members turn towards the entrance of the camp and watch as an all-white wolf runs into the camp towards them. On top of the wolf, rides a shadowy figure wearing a robe covering its entire body, revealing not an inch of its skin. The members continue to look on as the figure rides into the camp straight past all the guards. As the wolf gets to them it stops as everyone around watches with intent. With the group standing in silence, one of the nearby aides applying bandages upon the wounded turns swiftly to the approaching figure.

"Didn't I tell you I never wanted to see you again?" the aide says, lowering her hat and revealing a womanly face. The members turn their heads back and forth, watching suddenly as the figure lowers its cowl onto its back.

"The fact you're here is irrelevant to me. I came here for Shard," the figure replies. As his cowl settles onto his back, the weight shifts, allowing the members to spot a growing line of leather armor sneaking from underneath. They watch as the figure dismounts from the wolf as the aide approaches from the side. Stepping towards the wolf, she pushes the figure out of the way and grabs the icicles between the layers of fur. The aide snarls as she walks past the figure as the guild watches on in amusement.

"What do you think happened?" Mosenrath asks to Molozel. He watches as his eyes remain locked on to her flowing blonde hair.

"I don't know but she looks amazing," Molozel replies as Mosenrath's eyes jolt towards him.

"Endaersal, you know he never listens to anything anyone says," the aide says as she wipes some of the condensation off an icicle.

"I am so glad I don't have to care about what she says," Endaersal whispers.

"What is her name?" Molozel whispers at Endaersal's side.

"Annabella, but watch out with her rage," Endaersal replies, turning to him.

Annabella turns to Endaersal, and shakes her head before mounting up on the back of the wolf, avoiding all the icicles. "Come, Shard, lets go to the stable, and I'll cool you off." After a moment of hesitation, the wolf howls and charges away to the stable nearby.

Endaersal shakes his head angrily, then looks back at the guild, standing silently to the side. "What do you want?"

"Nothing really, we are just stopping here for a while until we head to Volzia," Tharxion replies.

"Why would you do this?" Endaersal asks.

"We have orders from Lord Kolozi that we are to strike the Barazul there," Tharxion answers, watching as the other members remain silent.

"May I come along the journey?" Endaersal asks.

"Certainly, we can always use more members," Tharxion replies, extending his hand out between them.

"So when do we leave?" Endaersal asks, shaking Tharxion's hand.

"Right now, but before you head off you must talk to Cheshete, our rogue leader," Tharxion replies, pointing over to one of the members as he twirls two daggers between his fingers.

Endaersal walks away towards Cheshete as the guild continues to approach a lone armored guard with a single scroll inside his gauntlet.

Cheshete spots Endaersal and stops to allow the members to get ahead of him. "Our role in the BloodMinazue is to bring forth blood and pain."

Endaersal nods his head, looking down at fresh set of daggers wrapping around his belt. He turns his attention back to Chesete, watching as he approaches his awaiting dragon. As Cheshete mounts up, Endaersal looks back at the town and watches as Annabella appears alongside Shard, heading deeper into the town. Endaersal then looks back and smirks at Cheshete who nods in return.

"Ready?" Cheshete asks.

"Let's go," Endaersal replies, watching as Cheshete takes off towards the horizon.

Endaersal steps up and looks at the guard who summons up a vortex. The dragon explodes out of it and lands in front of Endaersal, allowing him to jump on before it takes off behind Cheshete. As they continue to fly off towards their destination, they watch as the sun travels throughout the sky as the time passes by. After a while, they reach the rest of the group who is slowing down a bit to allow the rest to catch up. As the group is flying together, they reach the Silent Land's border into the more mountainous region of the Skyshatter Range. As the guild enters the land, they pass over the top of Camp Limano, which is the Minazue fortress in the valley of the mountainous land. A range of stone tents covers the open spaces between the trees. Passing above, the members look down at the fragmented remains of the town. As they leave it behind, the members fly through the peaks of nature's towers until they make it out into the valley section of the land. Flying through, Endaersal spots a small oasis below, and watches as the wildlife drinks the water

"That's probably the only pure place in this region," Nastale replies as he looks back to Endaersal.

Endaersal continues to watch it get farther away, and the border into the next land gets closer. As the members cross into the Topalazi, Tharxion looks back to the guild as they are looking for any sign of life.

"We're going to stop in Machizol, I have something to do here," Tharxion says.

"Also the trolls here can be slightly stubborn about their items," Narlugo says, looking back from his dragon.

"What happens if I anger one?" Mosenrath asks.

"Guards will banish you from the city," Narlugo replies. One by one, the members land as they dismount, allowing their dragos full reign of the mountainous terrain.

"The city of Machizol is one of the few towns in the Glacios where the inhabitants are able to build their own designs," Amadeas says.

"Yea, and supposedly they build their houses using parchment that travelers leave behind," Bulling replies. As the last member gets off their drago, the guild looks at the entrance to the town where they find Tharxion about to enter.

"Everyone can come in except for the Sybolisk, they have a special trader's lane for you," Tharxion says, turning back around.

"Yeah, you're too dangerous so we have set aside a place just for you," one guard replies, pointing his spear at an opening to the side of the entrance.

"You only did that because I wouldn't budge on my price," Necromyr replies. Placing his triton back on its holder, Necromyr watches as he turns to the others as black smoke swirls from off their bodies. Necromyr and the four other Sybolisk walk through the opening as the rest of the members walk inside, except for Bulling who just peeks inside, and then comes back to them outside.

"What's wrong, Bulling?" Nosferatmoo asks, turning back so Bulling can see his bovine features.

"Nothing, I just have some business in Turbinin Point," Bulling replies.

Nosferatmoo shrugs, watching as Bulling makes his way over to an open section of ground and stops in his tracks. He reaches inside his pant pocket and pulls out a large ruby, glowing with his touch. Nosferatmoo lifts his hoof to the stringy hair along his chin as he watches as Bulling lobs the ruby into a sand dune. After a moment, the swirling gust freezes in place as the sandy ground trembles all around them. From out of the sand, lava slides out from the top and descends onto the bottom, pillowing upwards as it takes shape. Taking the form of a creature few had seen, part beast and part elemental demon, this creature carries the name Molten Saber. Bearing the shape of a goliath saber tooth tiger, the beast's skin solidifies from lava into tar. They watch as Bulling mounts it as it releases a loud, hissing sound. Once he grabs hold of two loose portions along its frame, they take off toward the desert nearby toward Turbinin Point.

"What's wrong with him?" Tyrodris asks, following Bulling's path with his bluish eyes.

"I don't know, but something isn't right," Nosferatmoo replies, turning back as his ears twitch in the wind.

"Why don't you go check it out, we'll just be here messing around," Tyrodris says as he turns around to see Viraxx juggling some round fruits of different colors. Viraxx stops and looks back with a grin as he places the fruit back on the shelf as Tyrodris turns back to Nosferatmoo.

"Okay, then I guess I will go find out," Nosferatmoo replies. He turns with glowing eyes, stopping at the location where Bulling began his trek.

Suddenly, Nosferatmoo unleashes a mighty moo, causing a geyser of rock and soil to erupt from beneath the sand. As the shards slam into the ground, the ground trembles as a wolf-like creature explodes from the opening. Its paws and body made of chunks of earth, the beast slams its paws down with every step, leaving a trail of soil behind it. Unleashing a howl, the wolf stands in front of Nosferatmoo, allowing him to take the reins. With a single slap against its back, it takes off behind Bulling as Viraxx and Tyrodris remain standing outside the town.

***

Meanwhile, Bulling arrives at Turbinin to find the small shanty town to be deserted. "I know there is something here I can sense it."

His feet touch the ground just as his mount melts down through the sand, burning an outline in the earth. Bulling begins to examine the post, when he sees for a brief second a shadow on top of the crates near one of the vendors. He pulls out his crossbow and begins to walk deeper into the camp. He stops in the entrance of one of the vendors, spotting a troll's body lying on the floor in a pool of greenish blood. As he is standing there, out from the top of the crates a shadowy figure jumps at him with daggers aiming downwards.

Before the daggers can strike, Bulling rolls out of the way and aims his crossbow, catching sight of the figure's white eyes. Before the miscreant can make a move, Bulling fires a bolt, striking it as it goes crashing through the crates next to the vendor. Bulling then walks up to the broken crates and finds the body, the bolt between the layers of the figure's dark armor. Looking elsewhere, the silence is once again broken by an evil snicker from the shadows. As he turns around, he finds three human figures with bluish skin standing in front of him. He watches as the ones on the sides drop down, taking the shape of a lion as the hooded one in the center takes out daggers and points them at him. As Bulling moves away from the last drooling lion, he suddenly takes off into one of the shops, hearing the roars of the lions as they pounce forward.

Inside the crevices of light, Bulling sneaks behind a table as the lions charge inside with a bloodthirsty look in their eyes. One sniffs at the table, opening its jaws as it leaps off the ground and flies over the table. Just as it lands, Bulling slides away into the shadows, lifting a bolt from his quiver. As Bulling aims a shot, a whimper rings out from behind the table as a plume of snowflakes cyclones toward the roof. Bulling fires a shot, sending the other one through the back wall, and looks back to see the other lion frozen in ice behind the table. Smirking at his deed, Bulling looks over as the lion remains frozen with its mouth wide open.

Bulling walks over to the hole in the wall, and steps through it to look for the other figure. Finding no trace, he looks down at the dead lion when suddenly the figure reappears, striking him with the back end of both daggers, stunning him. As Bulling struggles to right his spinning world, the short figure chuckles as he circles out of Bulling's range. The figure stops and reaches beneath inside his brown vest, pulling out a crystal vial containing a flat green substance. Popping the cork, the figure looks over at Bulling as he tries to wipe his eyes.

"See, even something as small as a dwarf can take down a Minazue," the dwarf says, dropping his hood to reveal his reddish hair all over his face.

The dwarf then coats his daggers in the greenish liquid before tossing the vial back outside the doorway. The dwarf then takes aim at Bulling when, unbeknownst to him, a pool of demonic fluid appears and skeletal hands explode out and grab the dwarf, pulling him into its depths. In shock, Bulling watches as the pool dissipates and then reappears near the doorway, watching as the dwarf reappears in the pool in front of Nosferatmoo.

Nosferatmoo blocks the dwarf's daggers with his axe and then spins around, slicing the dwarf in half. He walks up to the dwarf's twitching corpse and pulls out a scroll from the depths of his robe. Kneeling, Nosferatmoo opens the scroll between his hooves and watches as a demonic energy encases the corpse. Once the energy is channeled inside the entire body, the corpse evaporates into the shadows, just as Bulling breaks free from the stun.

"You owe me one," Nosferatmoo says, getting back to his feet as he looks over at Bulling. As Nosferatmoo chuckles, suddenly the other lion explodes through the wall, landing onto Nosferatmoo as stones crash all around them. As the lion begins to maul Nosferatmoo, Bulling fires a bolt that sends it flying into the sand.

"Now we're even," Bulling replies as Nosferatmoo turns and watches the lion slide down the coast into the green river water.

Nosferatmoo then walks over to Bulling as he tries to wipe the dust off his bow's trigger. "Is this what you sensed over here?"

"Not all this action, but some yes," Bulling replies as he walks up, watching as his Molten Saber reappears from the burnt outline in the sand. Bulling mounts up, and watches as Nosferatmoo whistles as his wolf leaps from the hillside.

"Let's get out of here!" Bulling yells before taking off towards Turbinin.

Nosferatmoo takes off behind him, and together they dash through the sand towards Machizol.

Chapter Nine

B ack in Machizol, Viraxx and Tyrodris are sitting with their open bags in front of them when Viraxx spots the charging duo. Viraxx stands up just in time to see the remaining members of the guild step outside of town. "Bulling and Nosferatmoo are back." Watching, the two members arrive to the group, and dismount as their mounts return to the elements from which they had come from.

"Did everything go okay?" Tyrodris asks, standing back up as he places his armor properly over his rib fragments.

Bulling gently nods at Nosfetamoo before looking back at Tyrodris. "Yep, just the usual Barazul ambush, but do not worry we took care of them."

"Those fools will never learn," Necromyr chuckles.

Bulling laughs and then walks over to the entrance where he spots Mosenrath walking into an open hut with various items. "Hey, Mosenrath would you mind buying bolts for my crossbow?"

"Sure," Mosenrath replies simply as he walks past a quiver of bolts and arrows.

"Why, don't you have enough?" Viraxx asks.

"You can never have enough," Bulling replies, placing the cover back over the top of the quiver.

Inside the town, Mosenrath leaves the tradesman with a quiver of bolts hanging to his side as he heads over to a large tent in the center of town. As he walks toward it, a tiny creature comes up to him, shining blue scales on his face. Trying to get closer, the Grumbluk rolls in front of his path.

"Mosenrath, you got to help me," the Grumbluk says, stretching out its pencil-thin arms.

Mosenrath looks at the Grumbluk's face with a bit of confusion. "Who are you?"

"It's me Narlugo, Tharxion gave me some scroll to read and now I look like this," Narlugo replies, waving his hands back and forth.

Mosenrath then looks over at Tharxion, seeing him laughing with Yuskiocha by the town forge as they point in their direction. "Calm down, he just gave you a Scroll of the Trickster's Mind which will wear off soon." Watching as Narlugo nods, Mosenrath shakes his head and steps around before going inside the large tent.

Narlugo turns around, and shakes his scaly fist at them, watching as they continue to laugh.

Once through the opening, Mosenrath notices two members at a wooden table eating some food as a chef makes his way from the table. Mosenrath walks around the table, causing them to look up from their plates.

"Hey, Mosenrath come sit down with us," Elash says, grabbing hold of the giant turkey leg laying across his plate. Elash, a member of the same clan as Mosenrath, is of human heritage despite his massive limbs that he got from merging with one of the yaks on his farm. His draping robe hangs to the floor, the insignia hidden behind a layer of crumbs.

"Yeah man, come on, and enjoy this food with your pals," Thoranbuff says as he shoves his face into chunks of meat inside a bed of brown sauce.

Mosenrath sits down in front of the two as the butcher comes back with a plate of chunks for him as well.

"He gave us this because we told him we don't eat anything alive," Elash says.

As the three are finishing, the sheet in the doorway opens, Tharxion walking inside with Nastale and Canosan behind him. They make their way through the silent room before stopping inches from the table.

"Come, we are heading out," Tharxion says, looking at each of them.

"Yeah, so get up or I'll make you get up!" Canosan yells, causing the three to stare at him as they slurp one last chunk down their throats. Canosan watches as they explode out of their chairs and stare angrily in his direction.

"Foolish mage, Tharxion will not always be around," Elash replies, slamming his fist just shy of his plate. As they walk out with Nastale, Canosan turns to Tharxion, struggling to calm himself down.

"He's got you there," Tharxion says as he makes his way through the sheet of linen.

"Yeah well, I can take him," Canosan replies as he quickly walks behind Tharxion outside. As the guild leaves the camp, they spot the other members outside, sitting near the market waiting for them.

"So, what have you guys been up to?" Zen asks, shifting their attention towards the approaching group.

The two turn to Bulling as he finishes placing the final arrow inside his quiver. Bulling smirks as they shift their attention back to Zen.

"Well, Bulling here went to the Point and took care of a Barazul encounter," Viraxx replies, pulling out a tuft of fur.

"What happened?" Tharxion asks, shifting his attention to Bulling as he slides his quiver back over his shoulder.

"I was in Turbinin Point when they tried to ambush me, but luckily I had my crossbow with me," Bulling replies, tapping the crossbow along the wooden shaft.

"Good, I guess the Barazul are awaiting our arrival, so we should not keep them waiting any longer," Tharxion says, making his way along the town's wall until finally reaching the end. He takes another couple of steps before stopping, turning towards the rest of the guild as a dragon appears. "You guys coming?"

"So, what did you need from here?" Nastale whispers to Tharxion just as he attempts to mount up on the dragon's back.

"Kolozi gave me a side mission to complete since we were going to be in the area," Tharxion replies, looking down at him as his hands grab hold of the scales lining the dragon's back.

"Just wondering, you didn't say anything about it," Nastale replies, lifting his feet as they sink into the sand.

"It wasn't anything big so don't worry. Let's just go to Ancient

Gailm," Tharxion says as the dragon extends its wings causing Nastale to step back.

Nastale and the other members look on as Tharxion flies off into the swirling sky above leaving them behind.

Oxala shrugs his heavily padded shoulders and jumps onto his own dragon before taking off behind Tharxion.

Bloodystomp walks forward and whistles as he watches his dragon swirl around the clouds as it dives downward. Coming to a stop, the dragon lands, allowing Bloodystomp to mount up as he turns back to look at the others. "You guys coming?"

As he flies away, the rest get onto their own dragons and take off behind him toward the Ancient Gailm. Leaving the city behind them, the front of the group spots a massive ridge of snow-covered peaks bending about the rocky landscape. As the members' eyes catch sight of a single cave with dagger-like icicles covering all sides of the opening, Mernerva flies forward to the front of the group next to Tharxion.

"Hey man, so what are we going to do in Ancient Gailm?" Mernerva asks.

"I have no idea, but I'm sure we'll find out together," Tharxion replies, looking back to the horizon after briefly looking at Mernerva. As the two turn their attention towards the green land beyond the other side of the mountainous terrain another brutish member approaches Crusayder.

"Hey, aren't there rumors about ancient creatures inhabiting the Ancient Gailm?" Aarrg asks, shifting his orcish frame to regain some comfort amongst the dagger like scales beneath him.

"There certainly is, and it is said they enjoy the taste of orcish warriors," Crusayder replies with a chuckle.

"Yeah, so you better watch out or they might eat you," Madagno adds, turning his brown eyes towards them as his dragon continues forward.

Aarrg's eyes widen as he turns to Tharxion who looks back with a smirk as he shakes his head.

As the members continue to fly, their eyes shift upwards when suddenly a squad of prehistoric birds appear, their jaws hanging off the hinges. Their leathery wings extend outward as they fall with their talons aiming at the members invading their air space. Before the beasts can get any closer, Tharxion turns back and points upward as they nod, preparing for a defense. As the members begin to gather their scrolls, the beasts turn away from the members, allowing them to take their hands off the curled-up scrolls. The members then come up to the edge of the snowy land just as the sun is beginning to set over the horizon. Inside Ancient Gailm, the guild finds the landscape to be a complete contrast from where they just left. The members look around as they admire the sections of the elemental land. As the members head towards the camp in Ancient Gailm, they pass by the active volcano in the center of the elemental planes that make up the land.

"Is it me, or is there something wrong here?" Robilard asks, lifting his metallic helm, revealing his elvish traits.

"What do you mean?" Nastale replies, looking over the side of his dragon to see trees made of crystals throughout the greenery.

"Well, it looks to me like the camp is empty," Robilard replies, lifting his hand as he points out to a bundle of tents.

"How about you Visuvium?" Nastale asks, looking back at the dragon behind his own.

"You know what, I think he's right it does look empty," Visuvium says, keeping his eyes on the tents.

The members look down, as they get closer to the camp, continuing to find no trace of life. One by one, the members land, releasing their dragons to soar back above the clouds.

"Who are we looking for?" Molozel asks, squatting down as he runs his hand through the muddy soil.

"The Atinzia people who live here," Yuskiocha asks, stepping over him, leaving a footprint just shy of his hand.

"Yes, where are they?" Methyl asks, watching as Yuskiocha peels back a curtain before looking back at him.

"I don't know, but I'm sensing some humanoids inside there," Bulling replies as he points toward a moss-covered cave just beyond the group of tents.

The members slowly creep their way inside, when suddenly a chunk of the tree's roots snaps off and begins to walk towards them. Unable to speak, the group watches as it grows a set of arms along with stumpy legs, a head taking shape. Just as it gets to the other end of the tent, the creature opens a pair of brown eyes, taking in the sight of the group.

"What is that?" Mosenrath whispers, watching as another steps out from behind a thick row of bushes.

"It's a plant," Gunny replies.

"The exact term is Lomiazalo, or you can call me Lomia," the creature says as it begins to grow to human size.

"Okay Lomia, do you know where we can find the inhabitants of this place?" Tharxion asks.

Lomia nods and walks inside the cave as the members follow with some hesitation. The members head further inside, finding themselves surrounded by crystals of all elements which light up the walls of the cave. As the members continue following Lomia around a corner, their eyes catch sight of an old bridge with chains of algae hanging from each line of rope. They walk over, causing a screeching sound to echo from stone plates sliding into each other. As Bloodystomp and Oxala are walking over the bridge, a chunk of shadow breaks off and slams into them. As they slam into the wall the shadow balls up on top of the floor. Stopping the group in their tracks, they turn back to watch as it swells up and starts to take shape. Taking form, the glowing crystals reveal its grizzly, wolf-like appearance along with dangerous fangs. The creature's large white eyes turn their attention to the stunned members as they struggle to their feet.

"Lozin, NO!," Lomia yells, charging towards it as the rest of the members remain on the pathway. Watching as the beast's skin oozes into place, Lomia lifts his leaf hand, causing the creature to shift its glowing eyes, which stops the oozy beast from getting closer. Grumbling beneath its jagged teeth, the beast sits down as its tail curls around its frame. "It's okay Lozin, they're here to help."

Lozin howls, causing the room to shake, before sliding back into the shadowy depths and allowing the peace to return. As the members continue down into the cave, their eyes catch sight of a glowing wall and a figure lying at the foot of it. As the members cautiously approach the body, Lomia sinks his feet into the soil, and places his leaf-hand on the two arrows in the green skin on his chest.

"Is he Minazue or Barazul?" Oxala asks, struggling to take in the various plant features making up the unconscious body.

"It's one of us, his name is Valiat Morin," Lomia replies as his eyes remain shut, some of the leaves along his arms wilting to the ground.

"Lomia, is that you?' a voice mutters as the guildies look around the room for the source.

"Pomina? Is that you?" Lomia asks, opening his eyes as leaves begin to sprout from out of his arms.

"Aye, we are here, but I fear they got Valiat," Pomina replies.

"Yes, the Barazul killed him," Lomia says, looking down at the body as it begins to decompose into the ground. As his words resonate, sounds of sniffling echo around the room causing the group's attention to shift toward the wall.

"They killed him because he wouldn't join their army, and disobey the Atinzia oath," Pomina replies behind a veil of sadness.

"I'm so sorry, but how do we get you guys from out of there?" Lomia asks, lifting his feet from out of the ground. After a brief silence, the faint sound of whispering catches the guild's attention.

"I'm not sure," Pomina says.

Lomia then turns back to the members, and shrugs as they begin to look at one another for ideas. The members examine the wall, placing their hand along the jagged crystals along the wall's face, when they notice a hole at the bottom near where they had found Valiat.

"Anyone got any explosives?" Mosenrath asks, watching the group search their possessions.

"You do know that will blow everything up including us," Narlugo replies, lifting his face out from his backpack.

"Do you have any better ideas?" Mosenrath asks, focusing his attention on him.

"If you two don't stop, I'll leave you in the volcano!" Gunny yells.

Shaking their heads, Mosenrath and Narlugo both turn to Gunny before turning their attention back to the glowing wall. Mosenrath then turns to Tharxion, and then turns back for a second before turning back to Tharxion. "I have a better idea."

"What is it now?" Narlugo asks as the others pause what they are doing.

"Hey Tharxion, can't we just break the crystal wall down?"

Mosenrath asks.

Tharxion looks back at some of the members of his group in disbelief as they search their bags with a renewed purpose. Before long, Tharxion drops his hand and pulls out a morphic orange rock which molds inside Tharxion's hand.

"What is that thing?" Gunny asks.

"An Emberite, which can be used to melt down any item it is placed against," Mosenrath replies. The group watches as Tharxion drops his bag to the floor as he makes his way over to the foot of the wall.

"Greetings Pomina, it is I, Tharxion the Warmaster of the Blood-Minazue, and I'm wondering how many of you there are?" Tharxion asks, examining the wall.

"Well, there are five of us," Pomina replies.

"Okay then, this might work," Tharxion says, looking back as three others make their way to his side.

The group watches as they pull out their scrolls and begin to chant a spell as Tharxion places the Emberite into the wall. Watching as it molds into the crevice between crystals, Tharxion steps back as he continues his own casting.

"Hopefully they don't come out all messed up like the last person I was trying this on," Mezmur says, turning toward Tharxion who continues to keep his focus on the fluctuating wall.

"Okay, we're going to need some of you to help fully charge this thing," Tharxion says, looking back at the rest of the group.

Suddenly, members of all classes went to the Emberite, channeling their energies into the crystal, causing the wall to deteriorate. After a few moments, the crystals melt away a chunk around the Emberite, revealing another creature like Pomia on the other side.

"You did it!" Lomia says, lifting his leaves high into the air.

"Did you think it would fail?" Tharxion asks, watching as the hole extends all the way to the muddy floor.

Gathering in line, the plants cheer the group that had freed them when they stop to see Lomia hiding in Tharxion's shadow. Making their way over, Lomia greets them with a gentle wave of his leafy branch.

"Is it safe outside?" Pomina asks.

"Aye, it's as safe as it can ever be," Lomia replies.

Pomina turns to the others as they begin to cheer, running outside, except for one that turns back to look at the crumbling wall of crystals.

"Hey Elemgaite, you coming outside?" Lomia asks, turning his flowery head.

Elemgaite turns her head, and grins at Lomia before pulling a petal off her head. "You want me to leave and miss an opportunity like this."

Lomia watches as Elemgaite kneels and reaches the leaf down into the soil. Picking up a mixture of soil and broken crystals, Elemgaite folds up the leaf and places it inside one of the satchels around her neck.

Lomia then turns to the BloodMinazue as they begin to place themselves up against the wall, trying to rest themselves against the mossy surface. "My apologies, BloodMinazue, I had forgotten that you are still here."

"It's okay, we must be off anyway. We have an epic battle waiting for us," Nastale replies.

"You can't leave now! It's nighttime, and who knows what kind of danger is awaiting you outside," Lomia replies, pointing out into the darkening sky outside the cave.

"What kind of dangers?" Endaersal asks, turning toward the entrance with a firm grasp upon his silvery daggers.

"Well, you have the creatures that perch themselves along the volcanic cliffs, as well as the elemental creatures that roam between planes," Lomia replies, causing the rest of the BloodMinazue to look outside.

"Sounds dangerous," Gunny replies with a grin as he looks down at his gigantic sword.

"It truly is," Lomia says.

The members turn towards the entrance of the cave just as a lightning bolt lights up the entrance, revealing rain hidden by the darkness.

"I guess the Barazul can wait another day," Cappicola replies, placing his head up against the wall as his eyes shut.

"I guess you're right," Mernerva replies, sitting down next to him.

"Okay then, make yourself comfortable. This is the safest spot we have here," Lomia says.

The members separate as they walk around the cave in search of a comfortable place to relax. As each of the members begins to lie down, Baltor gets up and walks towards the entranceway. He gets to the edge of the falling rain before leaning himself against the rocky wall to watch as the rain as it continues, the plants collecting the water on their leaves. Suddenly, Baltor turns when a crack of lightning reveals a mysterious shadow between the group of plants. Taking a step forward, the shadow reappears after another bolt of lightning lights up the sky. As the thunder rumbles across the sky, the firefly lights around the cave light up, revealing the figure splitting the group as it marches up to the cave's entrance.

Unsure of what to do, Baltor struggles to grab hold of his sword's grip as he pulls it out, watching it come closer. Baltor turns back, spotting Tharxion who is laying down his scroll bag along a mushy pile of soil. "Tharxion, come quick, we have an intruder."

Tharxion turns towards him, and quickly gathers up his mace as he runs towards Baltor where he stops as he sees the figure passing the closest tent to the door.

Baltor looks back when suddenly he jumps backward, seeing the figure face-to-face with him.

"Greetings, are you the BloodMinazue guild?" the figure asks in a deep voice.

"That is us," Baltor mutters as he retreats towards Tharxion.

"I am Legorn and I come to you from Dapalos," the figure replies, dropping his soaked hood to reveal his elvish skin and the pair of blue eyes staring back at them. Legorn's wavy hair slides down behind his pointy ears as his skin bounces between colors to blend with the landscape. The rest of his body is hidden behind a black coat, revealing only the trim of a metal armor along the edges.

"Oh, then please come inside and out of this rain," Tharxion replies, motioning his hand as Legorn steps forward under the safety of the cave.

"I cannot stay because I am here to deliver a message from Lord Kolozi," Legorn says as he reaches inside one of his sleeves, pulling out a damp message. He hands the message over to Tharxion, who unrolls it before reading out aloud.

"If you are reading this then Master Kolozi requires a representative of the BloodMinazue in Dapalos immediately," Tharxion reads before rolling the letter back up.

"Farewell, mighty BloodMinazue, and Bleed well," Legorn says, lifting his hood back up as he walks into the rain, fading away from view.

"I'll go," Baltor says before anyone can speak.

"Okay then, hurry back because we shall be off at dusk," Tharxion replies.

Baltor walks over to his bag, pulling out a scroll and watching as it begins to glow multiple colors. After a second, Baltor disappears and Tharxion settles back down by his stuff.

Tthe night passes peacefully, the members waking up to a misty day and Tharxion wipes his eyes as he looks around for any sign of Baltor. "I see Baltor has yet to return," he says, stretching out as he gets back to his feet.

"Where did he go?" Thoranbuff asks, turning over toward the darkness of the cave.

"We got a letter from Kolozi last night while everyone was asleep," Tharxion replies.

"A letter from Kolozi surely seems important," Thoranbuff says, rolling onto his stomach as he places his hands onto the ground.

"Indeed, however it didn't say what he wanted," Tharxion replies as suddenly a burst of wind swirls inside.

"Not to interrupt you, but your friends have just flown in," Lomia says, watching as they turn their attention towards him. Just as Lomia finishes, Baltor appears alongside Molozel as they walk toward the cave. As they walk inside, the members look on in confusion as they stop gathering their supplies.

"I'm sure you're wondering what Molozel is doing here," Baltor says, watching as the group remains motionless.

"Now that you mention it, I do wonder," Mezmur says, brushing off his robe as he straightens back up.

"Well when I got to Dapalos I was met by Kolozi and Molozel, and Kolozi told me that Spirit Sanctuary had more bodies than they needed, so he thought we could use him," Baltor replies.

"Hey, if Kolozi thinks we can use him, then who are we to say no?" Oxala says, placing his staff onto his back.

The members nod their heads, finishing preparations as the two walk deeper into the cave. Molozel continues towards the heart of the cave as Baltor stops in front of Tharxion in the entrance. As Molozel walks past the members, he spots the crystal wall and Elemgaite gathering a sample of the crystal along the floor. "What happened here?"

"Barazul," Elemgaite says, keeping her focus on the sparkling shards in front of her.

"Damn cretins never let us live in peace," Molozel replies as his eyes twinkle with the crystal's reflection. As Molozel turns around to the guild, he spots Baltor calling him back to the front. Molozel nods, and heads back to the front where Tharxion and Baltor are standing.

"Greetings Molozel, we are about to head out to Volzia to fight the Barazul. Do you have any questions?" Tharxion asks, stopping Molozel in his tracks.

"No, just to look to find my place amongst your group," Molozel replies, looking around at the other members getting ready.

"Well, for that you need to talk to Stelton. He's the leader of your class," Tharxion says as he points out Stelton.

Molozel nods, and then walks over to Stelton as he tosses his warthog a piece of meat from his bag. "Warmaster Tharxion tells me I should talk to you about my role in this group."

"Indeed, well first thing I should ask is what is your strength?" Stelton asks, inspecting Molozel's weapons.

"Well I claim most of my kills with this," Molozel replies, looking down at his sword.

"Okay, where is your pet?" Stelton asks, looking around the ground.

"Over there," Molozel replies, pointing over to his warthog finishing up the last scrap of meat.

"That isn't tough enough. You need something like this," Stelton replies, snapping his finger.

Molozel looks around when something suddenly growls from the darkness as a vile creature steps out into the crystal light. Its dinosaur-like frame is covered in sections of bones missing all traces of muscles. Within its lips, two rows of sharp teeth mix with blood and saliva, which drip from its mouth.

Molozel's eyes widen in fear as he turns back to Stelton. "I definitely don't have one of those."

"Well then, we're going to have to get you one," Stelton says as he looks around at the crowd of members.

"How are we going to do that?" Molozel asks, watching as Stelton continues to look around.

"Bulling and Mosenrath, can you come here for a minute please," Stelton says, catching their attention.

Molozel turns his head to see Bulling and Mosenrath walking towards them as the others look on. As the two arrive, Stelton greets them and then turns to Molozel pointing out Bulling's pet.

"What's up, Stelton?" Mosenrath asks, looking around at the others.

"Can you and Bulling help Molozel try and get one of those crystal Elozaur?" Stelton asks as a loud roar shakes the cave.

"What is an Elozaur?" Molozel asks, looking outside as the others brace themselves.

"A prehistoric carnivore, made of a mixture of elemental crystals and lean flesh," Stelton replies. As Stelton finishes, the other members turn to him as everyone grows quiet.

Mosenrath and Bulling look at the other members, and then to turn to one another nodding their heads. "Yeah sure, let's do it, but I think we're going to need someone to save us in case we get into trouble," Mosenrath says.

Stelton nods his head and looks around the cave until he finds a pointy-eared blue figure meditating in his half white and half black robe. His hood slumps around his neck, hiding his face behind a layer of shadows.

"Hey Amadeas, would you mind helping them out?" Stelton asks, watching as the figure remains still against the wall.

Amadeas remains silent before suddenly opening his eyes with a glare towards Stelton as he gets up from the floor. "I don't mind, but next time say please."

"Alrighty well, go to the volcano and try to come back in one piece," Stelton replies, watching as Amadeas lifts himself up using the staff planted at his side.

"We won't promise anything," Bulling says, moving his arrows back and forth.

"Speak for yourself, I just had the leather in my armor repaired," Mosenrath says, brushing off some dust from his chest piece.

"Whatever, just go," Stelton says as he points to the entrance of the cave.

The group nods and walks out of the cave in search for any sign of Elozaur tracks. They watch as Lomia approaches them with a couple of horses made from local plant life. After two get onto each one, Bulling looks around as Lomia heads back over to his own tent. As the group is about to take off, Pomina appears from behind the bushes and walks up to the side of Amadeas.

"Are you guys looking for a Crystal Elozaur?" Pomina asks, placing his hand on the back of the horse.

"Yes we are," Amadeas replies, looking back at Pomina as she looks around the tent site.

"I thought so, well I saw one in the trees just outside of the Blazing Forest," Pomina says as he turns around and quickly jumps back behind the bushes.

Amadeas turns back to the other group members and points in the direction of a section of trees in an everlasting inferno. He then places his hand on the side of the horse and looks back just as he takes off in its direction. The others take off behind Amadeas, trying to stay out of the nearby swamp to avoid any conflict with the undead creatures that call it home. As the group continues to ride past the different inhabitants of the land, suddenly Bulling comes to a stop. The others stop as well before retreating to Bulling just as he dismounts from his horse, looking at the trees bustling in the wind.

"What's up?" Molozel asks. He and the others dismount as their horses begin to look around.

"Come over to me and be silent," Bulling whispers as suddenly the plants ahead shake violently.

They turn around as the ground begins to tremble and a herd of glowing deers jumps from out of the tops of the bushes. From out of the row of the trees ahead, a Crystal Elozaur appears into view, letting out a roar that chills the members' blood. Bulling gulps, and then looks back at the group, whose eyes are fixated upon the Elozaur.

"Alrighty, the plan is for me to lay out a trap for the beast to give Molozel some time to do his stuff," Bulling says.

The others nod and look back at the Elozaur while Bulling sneaks forward, using the brush for cover. Bulling stops after a bit and then turns back to the others. The three sneak towards Bulling as Bulling peeks from behind the tree to look in front of him. After the others arrive, Bulling storms from behind the tree and quickly buries a glowing seed within the grass in front of the Elozaur. Bulling looks up when suddenly the Elozaur starts to charge towards him, forcing him behind a tree.

"Go!" Bulling yells as massive vines begin to wrap around the Elozaur's crystalline legs. The group runs towards the struggling dinosaur, and stops as Molozel pulls out a cracked ruby egg.

Just as the egg begins to glow, the dinosaur begins to gnaw at the vines, and then turns its focus on Molozel. Before the dinosaur can attack, the dinosaur suddenly stops when massive vines appear below it, entangling the creature's body.

"Are you almost done?" Amadeas asks, poking his head out from behind one of the trees.

"One second," Molozel replies. Molozel stops as they watch the Elozaur disappear and the crack on the egg seals up with a greenish aura. After a moment, the egg shoots a green light, creating a smaller version of the Elozaur on top of the grass besides Molozel. The group looks down at the Elozaur and then back up at Molozel as he continues to watch the creature look at his surroundings.

"So, what are you going to name it?" Bulling asks.

Molozel turns to the Elozaur as it gnaws on a section of grass as the perfect name comes to him. "Its name is Ravager." Molozel watches as the Elozaur lifts its head from the crystal egg shells surrounding it.

Ravager walks over to Molozel's side and begins to look around while the members mount back up. Molozel looks over at the crystal casing and lifts it up before throwing it into the bushes nearby.

"Let's go back to the cave so we can show off Molozel's new pet," Mosenrath says.

The others nod their heads, and as they are mounting up a darkness overtakes the light in the sky. As they look up, a swarm of phoenix birds rise from the volcano's crater, leaving behind a trail of falling lava. Forming a line, the birds head for the group as their golden beaks straighten out in the wind.

"Those are Molten Aerioz!" Bulling yells, pointing at the incoming birds.

"What should we do now?" Mosenrath says, looking down at Bulling.

"We need to get out of here," Bulling replies as he takes off in the other direction.

Mosenrath turns back to Molozel as he takes his place behind him as Ravager sits in his lap. Once he was secure, Mosenrath takes off behind Bulling as the Aerioz let out a shrill cry, unleashing a dive upon them. With the Aerioz getting closer, the group rides away, dodging the trees, and bushes that are standing in their way. The group passes the final row of trees into a clear area, when suddenly Bulling spots a cave along the cliffside in front of them. As they continue to ride, Mosenrath turns to look back as suddenly one of the Aerioz dives and lands just short of the horse's tail. Mosenrath turns back and catches up to Bulling just as they are about to reach the cave. As the group reaches the entrance, the Aerioz suddenly stop at the edge of the Blazing Forest and turn back.

Chapter Ten

Trotting around the lip of the opening, Bulling dismounts as his eyes focus on the darkness inside the cave. Bulling enters the cave with his hand firm on his sword's handle, walking deeper inside the cave as he leaves the sight of the others. "Tharxion, Stelton, Is anyone there?"

Reaching a point where the light cannot break the depths of the darkness, Bulling finds himself surrounded by cold walls with no sign of the exit. Bulling stops in the darkness, struggling to listen for any sounds which may lead him back outside. As he looks around, suddenly something drips onto his boot causing his eyes to bolt toward his feet. Bulling kneels, but quickly jumps back when a growl begins to echo throughout the cave. Taking a step back, Bulling turns around when suddenly two red eyes appear from out of the darkness. Gasping for a breath, Bulling steps back, pulling out an arrow with a glowing tip, revealing an ape-like creature. Made of earth and rock, the creature reveals fangs of hard rock as its tongue waves back and forth. Craving flesh, the creature slams its muscular fists against its chest.

"I thought Plimapes to be nothing but myth," Bulling mumbles as he retreats, kicking pebbles out of the way.

The Plimape quickly backs out of the light, growling from the darkness. Suddenly, the Plimape reappears, but this time two others step out alongside it.

Bulling's eyes widen as he turns around and drops the arrow onto the stony floor. As he runs away, the Plimapes sink back into the darkness, watching as the light gives out, allowing the darkness to take full control.

As Bulling reaches the outside, his eyes widen as he runs into the other members as they approach the cave's entrance.

"What's the matter?" Molozel asks, stopping as he watches Bulling charge forward.

"It's the wrong cave," Bulling replies, sliding to a stop as he tries to catch his breath.

Amadeas and Mosenrath turn to one another as a smirks begin to creep onto their faces. Their smirks turn into smiles and then into a chuckle as Bulling and Molozel watch on, unsure of what is so funny.

"We knew that, we just wanted to see you go inside," Amadeas says, wiping the tears from his eyes. The two begin to laugh again as Bulling begins to slowly pull his crossbow from off his back.

"Are you serious? I could've been killed," Bulling replies, struggling to keep from firing a bolt at them.

"Yep and you should have seen your face," Mosenrath says as he begins to mock the way Bulling was running away. As the group is watching Mosenrath, a bolt suddenly strikes the ground near his feet, stopping Mosenrath in his tracks. "What did you do that for?"

"I thought it would be fun," Bulling replies as he attaches the crossbow into the tangled web of vines making up the horse's figure.

"Where did you get a crossbow anyway?" Amadeas asks, mounting into place just above Bulling.

"None of your business. Just know that I have one," Bulling replies as the last vine hides the final trace of the weapon.

The group gathers their stuff as they mount back up on their rides to try to find the rest of the BloodMinazue. The group rides west in search of the cave, staying on the border of the different areas even as animal sounds echo around them. As the party continues, they arrive successfully at the swamp that lies at the foot of the camp. Making their way up the ramp, they find the guild outside, placing their belongings upon their own earthen steeds, preparing for the trip ahead. As they begin to approach the members, Tharxion looks up at them just as he finishes up.

"Welcome back, and congratulations on the new pet Molozel," Tharxion says, causing the other members to look up from what they were doing.

"Thank you," Molozel replies, throwing a morsel of meal at Ravager.

Joining the group, Lomia walks towards them as he leaves his spot by the cave's entrance. "Is everything ready for your journey?"

"It is, and we are ready to defeat the enemy once and for all," Tharxion replies, sending the entire guild into a roaring frenzy.

"Fantastic, now I must inform you that Minazue in the area have seen Barazuls heading from Solamid back into Ancient Gailm," Lomia says, pointing over to a sloping ramp along the hillside.

"Interesting, but no matter. We shall not make them wait for us any longer," Gunny replies, lifting his sword into the air.

"Yeah, I think we should show them the true power of the Minazue," Visuvium says as he looks over to Gunny.

"Indeed, mighty BloodMinazue may you travel with the blessing of all Minazue," Lomia says as he sprinkles broken leaves along the path.

The members roar as they raise their weapons in the air, one by one taking off down the ramp and away from the campsite. As the members leave, Lomia walks back over to his space where he finds Elemgaite running into the cave with a colorful crystal in hand.

As the members ride towards the opening which connects the lands, they look around at the crystal beasts grazing about. Making their approach, their eyes catch sight of the path as it curves through the mountainous terrain that borders the entire side of the land. Continuing forward, Tharxion rides up to the front when he spots a figure running down the road, continuing to look back behind it.

"Is he one of ours?" Thoranbuff asks, keeping his eyes on the being.

"I'm not sure," Tharxion replies as he rides past Thoranbluff and closer to the figure to get a better look. As the members follow, they stop as the figure continues to run towards them out of Volzia. The guild looks on as the figure runs up to Tharxion's mount out of breath and slightly jittery.

"You got to help me, they're chasing me," the figure says, eyes darting about the area.

"Who's chasing you?" Tharxion asks.

Before the figure can reply, a whistling sound zips past Tharxion's ears and the figure gasps as he falls to the ground.

Tharxion's eyes widen in shock, finding an arrow stuck in the being's back. The members dismount from their rides before pulling out their weapons, looking around the hillside.

Suddenly, Crimpste locates a familiar-looking Barazul, recognizing him as one of those that attacked the mage camp. Crimpste angrily stands with his hand hanging above his wand as the members try to search the crevices. Crimpste turns to Apocol and the other mages as they continue their search.

"The Barazul from the camp is up there!"

As they find the hiding Barazul, their eyes widen when they spot him grinning as he drops his bow to the ground. The rest of the guild turns to Crimpste, who suddenly pulls out a scroll, unleashing a fireball that explodes into the hillside. As the smoke fades, they find a burnt body on the ground, looking up at the hole where he was once standing.

He then turns back to the guild, watching as the anger begins to grow at the thought of their failure. He pulls out his sword as suddenly, out of the cliff, four more jump down and stand by his side. The Barazuls begin to charge them, when suddenly a barrage of streaking fireballs strikes them down. The BloodMinazue turn to find a group standing on the cliff, placing their scrolls away. The group jumps down as they inspect the guild, looking at their armor and crest. After a while, the figure in the center steps forward, along with an elven woman, both of whom stare cautiously at the members.

As the members watch, Methyl storms past Tharxion, rushing toward the two. As Methyl gets in front, the heavily armored man pulls out his sword, stopping Methyl in his tracks. The guild retaliates, grabbing their weapons as they watch the other group grab for their own.

"You are intruding on to the lands of Volzia and the lands of our fathers!" the man roars, keeping the tip of his blade against Methyl's neck.

The guild walks towards the group as Tharxion and Nastale take the lead.

"Excuse us, we mean no intrusion but we do require entrance to Volzia so we may extinguish the Barazul threat," Nastale replies, watching as Methyl's eyes cross at the sight of his shining blade. The leader lowers his sword enough to allow Methyl to step back toward the guild.

"Impossible, the Barazul have not impeded in these lands in years," the man says, turning to the woman.

"Indeed, but now they want to get rid of all Minazue for total control of Glacios," Tharxion replies, watching as the man turns his head back.

"If that is so, then who sends you here?" the leader asks, placing his sword closer to his side.

"Elder Kolozi and the Minazue Syndicate have sent us, so we may strike down the Barazul threat," Tharxion replies.

As Tharxion finishes speaking, the woman's silvery eyes widen as she turns her attention to the leader. She leans over, whispering something which turns the leader's expression a bit more favorable.

"My apologies, let me introduce myself, my name is Captain Salordra of the Dragon Raiders," Salordra replies, bowing his head. The guild watches as the group behind Salordra bow as well.

"Indeed, we are on our way to Nomaz Crown in order to meet a friend of ours who goes by the name of Narrava," Methyl says.

Salordra looks over at the woman before turning back to the guild. "Does Narrava mend and use seeds of the earth?"

"She does," Tharxion says, looking over at Methyl.

Salordra turns back to his group, and motions two of the three hooded figures forward. "My friends Wurmwood and Drokam found her and took her prisoner because of her hostility towards her fellow Minazue members."

"You took her prisoner?" Methyl yells, flexing his muscles as his hand sways over his weapon.

"Indeed, and our plan is to desert her in one of the pits inside Volzia," Salordra replies, gripping his weapon tightly.

"You will do no such thing, or you shall face the force of my staff," Methyl says, lifting his staff off his back before jamming it into the ground.

Salordra's eyes look down at the bamboo staff, which barely made an indent in the rocky ground. "You dare mock me in front of my second in command? I shall make you eat those words." As Methyl drops back, Salordra pulls his large shield off his back and places it alongside the giant sword. The two step forward with their weapons ready as the others watch on to see who will deal the first blow. Salordra charges forward with his sword in the air and, to the shock of the others, takes a swing in his direction.

Methyl pushes the sword downward with his hand before tripping Salordra with the edge of his staff. Salordra pushes himself back to his feet, looking down at his armor as dirt rains toward the ground. Salordra turns to Methyl as he stands in front of him, using his shield to send Methyl crumbling to the ground. As he tries to prop himself up, Methyl looks up to see Salordra looking down at him with a massive grin on his face and weapons to his side. As Methyl rises to his feet, Tharxion and the guild look on, when Gunny steps next to Tharxion.

"Are you going to stop this?" whispers Gunny.

"I should to save time, however, battles like these always humor me," Tharxion says, looking back at Gunny.

"Just end this already," Gunny roars, slamming his metal boot on top of Tharxion's bare foot.

"Fine I will," Tharxion replies, stepping forward as he tries to ignore the pain in his front.

At the same time, the woman steps forward, staring a hole through Tharxion. The woman turns to the three Minazue behind her, pointing in the direction of Salordra and Methyl. The guild looks on as Drokam and an orc hiding behind a thick robe step forward and head towards the fight. The two walk up to the combatants, grabbing hold of Salordra before dragging him back to the woman as she turns her attention to him.

"What are you doing? I was about to finish him," Salordra whimpers, kicking up some of the dirt into the air.

"Oh, please. You are no closer to impressing me than you are to finishing him," the woman replies, shaking her head.

"Come on, Anadae, you know his puny weapons wouldn't have left a mark," Salordra says, his fist pounding his metal chest plate.

"Yeah and his scrolls?" the orc asks, dropping his hood to reveal his greenish skin and protruding tusks.

"Octegra, this doesn't concern you, so stay out of it!" Salordra yells, struggling against them.

"Oh yeah?" Octegra says as his eyes darken.

Salordra lifts his sword high as he screams before charging him. He gets closer and as he is about to grab hold of Octegra, suddenly three arrows strike the face of the rocks between them.

Octegra and Salordra turn to see Yuskiocha standing still, his bow lowering back to his side.

"Thank you Yuski," Tharxion says, saluting Yuskiocha who steps back into formation.

Salordra angrily walks over to Anadae as Octegra brushes his robe off before heading between Drokam and Wurmwood.

"Well, your friend is inside our base nearby," Salordra mutters, glaring at the ground.

"Then we shall head there, and you shall free her," Methyl replies, placing the staff back on his back.

"I shall do no such thing," Salordra says, lifting his face up as anger reddens his eyes.

"What is stopping you?" Necromyr asks.

"Well you see, your Narrava is in love with a friend of ours," Salordra replies as he points to the top of the hill.

The members look up, seeing an armored figure atop a horse as the gusty winds blow his cape into the air. his body is of a reddish complexion, covered in a mixture of leather and woolen armor, his bluish hair slumping down the back of his neck.

"I thought you said she was your prisoner?" Nastale says, turning back to Salordra.

"She is, and when she's exiled he will be our lone wolf once more," Salordra replies, turning back as the figure rides out of sight.

"How far up the road is this camp of yours?" Molozel asks, looking toward the road.

"Just up the road, but we cannot assist you with any supplies because we dare not choose a side in this battle," Anadae replies before snapping her fingers.

The guild watches as the air behind Anadae twists and turns and suddenly a swirling portal appears, allowing the group to jump inside.

"Choose a side, the Barazul won't care when they destroy your camp," Cheshete says, watching as Anadae steps inside, leaving Salordra alone.

"When that day comes then we will decide, but for now we shall stay the way we are," Salordra replies before stepping inside the portal, leaving the group alone on their journey. Before any of them can make a move, the portal disintegrates, forcing the guild to turn their attention back to their horses.

Mosenrath mounts up first before riding toward the front of the group where he comes to a stop. "So, what are we waiting for?"

"Nothing, but they are going to expect us to follow them," Blucor replies, getting onto his own horse.

"Then we shall do it quietly," Narlugo says, pulling himself onto his horse's back. The rest of the members do the same, leaving Tharxion and Methyl standing alone.

"Methyl, don't you want to get Narrava back?" Mosenrath asks, causing Methyl to turn his attention to Tharxion.

"Yeah, and Tharxion, where is your leadership?" Bulling asks, shifting Tharxion's attention to him.

"Sort of, but not if she wants to stay with someone she loves," Methyl replies, wiping a rogue tear from his cheek. Mosenrath looks down at him, shaking his head in disgust as Methyl's eyes wells with tears.

"How dare you question my leadership skills? Sorry if I need everyone here to defeat the growing army," Tharxion replies, mounting up to join the others. With all the members looking at him, Methyl remains with his horse by his side.

"Are you coming?" Endaersal asks.

Methyl looks up, using his elbow guard to wipe away the moisture along his chin before shaking his head. "I can't do it." Methyl then pulls his horse forward, jumping on before taking off through an opening nearby.

"Shall we go after him?" Stelton asks, turning his head toward Tharxion.

"No, I believe he will come when he's ready," Tharxion replies as he takes off down the open road.

The guild nods, turning their mounts around as they take off behind Tharxion. As the guild rides toward the camp, the smell of burning cinders fills the air, smoke hindering their sight. In the distance they see the group's camp to the left of the road. The guild stops in a clearing just shy of the camp, hiding out of view, allowing Tharxion to turn to Endaersal and Blucor.

"I need you two to scope out the area," Tharxion whispers, pointing out the camp just beyond the boulders.

The two nod their heads and jump from their horses, allowing Tharxion to grab hold of their reins. They slowly make their way to the other side of the rocks as the rest of the group gather up behind the line of rocks. Looking inside, Salordra and Anadae sit beneath the main tent in the center, with Narrava kneeling in front of them, placing glowing seeds along the cuts on Salordra's arms. Struggling to keep her skin clean, Navarra wears a tan robe which hides her skin and her black hair which hangs over the hood. Her head turns to reveal her humanish face despite the green tint of her skin.

"See Anadae, I told you we could find use for this intruder," Salordra says, slamming his sword into the ground, causing Navarra to shift her attention.

Narrava looks back, absorbing the seeds as Salordra's skin seals up, and then quickly looks back down.

"I still think we should have given her to that guild," Anadae replies as she looks down at Narrava. As she finishes speaking, Narrava looks up with a glimmer in her eyes as Anadae's words ring through her ears.

Salordra kicks her off and rises to his feet as he turns back to Anadae."If we were to do that then Mortigillus will leave here, and we require his power." They look over at Mortigillus as he sharpens the blade of his dagger.

Mortigillus stares back as the glow of the flames brighten his bones and the darkness in his eyes when his hands freeze in the air. He gets up and walks over to his horse, placing his dagger back into its sheath of flesh.

Endaersal turns to Blucor as the two turn their attention toward the rest of the group. "She's in there."

As the members are about to step forward, suddenly a pair of demonic claws appear from behind the unsuspecting duo. The claws tear holes through their armor and drag them into the darkness as the others watch on helplessly. In disbelief, the members run up behind the wall and peek around to see the two now in front of Salordra, a demonic machine at their back. A twisted mess of darkness and mechanical parts, the monster's red eyes stare a hole through them as its hands reattach back into their joints. Salordra looks at Narrava and then glares back at the two as their keep their eyes on the ground.

"You dare try to sneak up on us? My Mana Breaker sees all," Salordra yells, lifting himself off his wooden throne.

As the members look on, Stelton and another grab hold of their bows, taking aim. Tharxion shakes his finger to still them, even as his hands unleash a purplish glow.

As Salordra walks over to the two with his sword in hand, he stops in front of Octegra and the towering Mana Breaker.

"What is it?" Octegra asks.

"I want you to order your pet to destroy these two," Salordra commands, pointing toward Blucor and Endaersal.

Octegra nods his head and then turns to the Mana Breaker, which takes a massive step toward the men. Its eyes lock on the men and its sword swings around its body before rising into the evening sky. It stops between them as the sword freezes horizontally in the air. Just as the Mana Breaker is about to attack, the demon's eyes suddenly turn green, freezing it and all its limbs.

"You can't even control your own demon, what kind of sorcerer are you?" Salordra chuckles, turning to Octegra.

The Mana Breaker suddenly grabs the sword and swings it at the burning chains between Blucor and Endaersal, freeing them.

Salordra retreats as, from the entrance, Tharxion appears with the members charging behind. Desperate, Salordra looks to Mortigillus, watching as he mounts up, and rides off into the darkness. Alone, Salordra looks back as the members enter the camp, and battle the few poorly armored guards standing in their way.

The Mana Breaker turns to Salordra, watching as he cowers behind his throne. As Salordra tucks himself behind the chair, the

Mana Breaker jumps toward the chair and throws it out of the way. Salordra scurries backward as the Mana Breaker closes the distance. Before the Mana Breaker can proceed, Octegra regains control, causing it to turn its attention toward the BloodMinazue.

"Salordra, shall we fight them or retreat?" Wurmwood asks, turning to Tharxion as he unleashes a pulse into one of the guards.

Salordra turns to Wurmwood and Drokam as they are fighting off the attacks of the guilds. As Salordra processes his options, Tharxion looks on from the other side of the battlefield, taking in the violence.

Nearby, Gunny strikes a guard with the blunt edge of his sword before looking over at Tharxion. "What shall we do Tharxion?"

Tharxion looks over the battlefield as Gunny kicks the guard over into the sand. "We shall stop this now and save our strength for the Barazul."

"Are you sure?" Stelton asks, knocking over a guard.

"Yes, I can't allow our brothers out there to fight any longer, especially with the Barazul waiting at full strength," Tharxion replies, watching as Stelton kicks the guard down in a heap. As the three look on, they watch as either sides fails to gain an advantage as the fatigue of battle settles in.

"Halt your battles!" Salordra and Tharxion yell in unison.

As the action ceases, both sides pick themselves up as the two walk toward the burning campfire. As both Salordra and Tharxion pass through, whispers turn to silence, causing the crackling flames to be the only sound to be heard. Salordra and Tharxion arrive at the fire where Anadae and her shadow stand, waiting with her arms crossed. As the three stand around, everyone takes their places within the shadows of the warm night.

"What is the meaning of this?" Anadae asks, looking at both men.

"They were trying to steal from us," Salordra replies to Tharxion's disgust.

"Steal from you, it's more like get back a friend that you have hostage," Tharxion says, pointing to Narrava as she stands alone inside a cage.

"Is that it?" Anadae asks, stomping her feet as she walks over to the cage and unlocks the door.

"What the hell do you think you're doing?" Salordra asks, throwing his arms up in the air.

"Ending this," Anadae replies, opening the door, allowing Narrava to step out of the confines.

Narrava walks out cautiously as she heads toward Tharxion and the others.

Salordra turns to Narrava before looking back at Tharxion and Anadae. "Now that you have your friend, you shall leave our camp and never return to it."

"Fine with me and, by the way, we could have easily destroyed you," Tharxion replies, making his way back to his friends.

Before Salordra can speak, Methyl appears at the edge of the light, dragging Mortigillus by his fleshy collarbone. "Hey, are you missing someone?" Methyl asks, making his way forward as Tharxion turns back to Salordra.

Salordra looks at Methyl and then at Mortigillus, his eyes trembling at the sight of his fallen comrade. "What did you do to him?"

"Relax, he's not dead," Methyl replies, continuing his trek into the camp. Methyl passes by Narrava, who sees Mortigillus, kneeling at his body.

"Are you okay?" Narrava whimpers, placing her hand against the rotting flesh of Mortigillus's skull.

Methyl looks with a frown, dropping the body as he walks toward Tharxion.

Narrava stares into the reflective bones of Mortigillus's face as a tear rolls down her cheek, puddling in a divot along the bridge of his nose. As the tears roll off his skull, Mortigillus's ribcage moves as he turns toward Narrava.

"What's wrong?" Mortigillus asks, Narrava weeping at his side.

"Nothing…nothing at all," Narrava replies as she wipes her eyes.

Mortigillus struggles to his feet but pauses, realizing he is the center of attention. As he gets to his feet, he stumbles over to Salordra and Anadae.

"What happened to you?" Salordra whispers.

"I don't remember, all I can remember is I was riding off, when there was a roar and then I was here," Mortigillus replies, placing his hand onto his fleshy forehead. As Mortigillus finishes, Methyl shrugs as everyone turns toward him.

"I thought you were leaving," Emerie whispers past his heavy facial hair to Methyl.

"I was, but then I saw him, and something just took over," Methyl whispers back.

Emerie nods before turning around to see Tharxion and Amadeas listening in on their conversation. "What did I do?"

Tharxion shakes his head, looking back at Mortigillus who continues to rub his head. "We dare not intrude any longer than we have, so we shall be off." With a snap of his fingers, the BloodMinazue turns around before moving toward the road.

"You're going to leave now? At the brink of night?" Salordra replies, pointing up at the lone crescent moon.

"The BloodMinazue is not scared to attack the Barazul in the night," Tharxion replies, listening as the others whisper around him.

"Do you even know where to go?" Drokam asks as he picks up some of the pieces of the broken chair.

"I hate to admit it, but my friend is right," Salordra says as he points to the edge of darkness where a pillar of smoke turns about.

The members look at one another until Gunny whispers something into Tharxion's ear.

Tharxion nods his head as he turns back toward Salordra and Anadae awaiting patiently. "We shall stay here the night, so we may be rested for our battle."

"That's a good idea," Salordra says, looking around the camp.

"Yes, now please sleep and don't worry. Our guards can watch the post," Anadae replies, watching as the guards take their posts among the wooden crates.

The guild breaks off, spreading out in search for somewhere to sleep.

As he looks on, Salordra turns to Mortigillus and Anadae both watching as the guild disperses. "Make sure they don't pull anything," he whispers.

"Consider it done," Mortigillus replies, getting up on his horse's back.

As the two leave, Salordra turns to the reddish smoke in the sky, shaking his head before walking to his tent. After some time, the smoke dissipates, much to the surprise of Tharxion and Crimpste as they sit on the wooden roof, watching the struggling flames on the horizon.

"Come morning, the blood of the Barazul shall coat our weapons," Crimpste says, tightening his hands on the fronds of the roof.

Tharxion turns to him as the rage in Crimpste's eyes flashes him back to the ambush at the camp. "By the way, you never told me what happened at the mage camp," Tharxion replies, breaking Crimpste's empty stare.

"I'd rather not relive the pain from that fateful night," Crimpste says as a tear falls onto the roof to his side.

"Don't worry, friend, they shall pay for those we have lost," Tharxion replies before placing his hand on Crimpste's shoulder. As the two watch the last cinders extinguish in the night, suddenly a creak breaks the silence. They quickly turn, looking at the edge of the light, where a familiar friend appears.

"What's going on up here?" Lukain asks as she takes a seat between the two.

"Nothing, just sitting here preparing for the battle tomorrow," Tharxion replies, looking over at the fading smoke.

"Yes, and I can say that it will be a victorious one," Lukain says, looking up at the stars sneaking in between the clouds.

"I hope so, for our sake, as well as the Minazue," Crimpste replies, looking down at the scars along his hands.

Lukain and Tharxion nod in agreement, turning their attention toward the tranquil surroundings. As the three sit in silence, suddenly from out of the shadows a figure tackles Tharxion off the roof, sending him crashing into a bundle of crates. The entire camp gathers up to see the commotion as Crimpste and Lukain look on in disbelief from the rooftop. Confusion covers their faces as they see a mysterious figure standing over Tharxion's prone body.

Chapter Eleven

Yuskiocha and Narlugo push their way to the front of the group, seeing the scene before them. The figure looks up from Tharxion, revealing the whites of his eyes. Yuskiocha pulls his bow from his back as the figure steps off to Tharxion's side.

"Wait!" Salordra yells, stepping between them and toward the figure.

As the group watches on, the figure stands still, watching as Salordra approaches him with caution. Salordra gets face-to-face with him, peeking inside the figure's hood, causing a smirk to extend on his face.

"Tell me why I shouldn't shoot a hole through this guy?" Yuskiocha yells, pulling back the quiver on his bow.

"It's Thorarin," Salordra replies, pulling down the hood, revealing a green face with scars from his cheekbone to his eyebrow.

Yuskiocha and Narlugo watch with their weapons at the ready as Anadae and Octegra walk around them, pushing their weapons down.

"I'm sorry about your friend, but I thought he was an intruder into the camp," Thorarin says, looking back down at the body in the center of the ruins.

"So, you tackled him through a chair?!" Narlugo yells, watching Amadeas and Emerie walk toward the body and pass Thorarin. The two kneel on both sides of Tharxion, and then look up at each other with a grim look on their faces.

"Can he be resurrected?" Molozel asks, looking at Narlugo and Yuskiocha.

"I believe so, however we don't know if his spirit is still in his body, so it's no guarantee," Emerie replies, staring into Amadeas's face. The two ruffle through their bags, eyes widening as their hands stop their search.

"We don't have anything to resurrect him with," Amadeas says, dumping out the random shreds of parchment inside his bag.

"Please tell me you're kidding," Yuskiocha replies, tears escaping from his eyes.

"Didn't you buy supplies from the scrollmaster in Dapalos?" Bulling asks.

The two priests scratch their heads, looking at each other before turning back to the guild unsure how to reply. "We didn't because we didn't think we needed any," Emerie replies, looking down at Tharxion.

The look of despair on Yuskiocha's face shifts to anger as he drops his bow onto the floor, turning to Emerie and Amadeas. "Damn healers, you can't do anything right!"

Yuskoicha then pulls out a javelin from underneath his cloak and aims it at the two men. Before he can charge forward, Visuvium and Forgarr catch his arms, dragging him behind a couple lines of guildies.

"I can resurrect him," Molozel says, stepping out of the group.

"How can you bring him back?" Thorarin asks, watching as Molozel pauses in front of the group.

"It's simple when you have this thing," Molozel replies, pulling a glowing arrow from out of his quiver. Molozel then kneels besides the body as Amadeas and Emerie back away. He takes a deep breath, lifting the arrow into the air and slamming it down into Tharxion, releasing a charge into his body.

"Was it successful?" Gunny asks, keeping his eyes on Tharxion.

Molozel gets up and then turns to the members, looking on in anticipation. "I guess we'll find out if it did."

"Wow, someone has faith in his items," Canosan replies, rummaging through a tiny satchel along his belt.

Before Molozel can respond, Tharxion's body begins to glow, and then stops as they look on from afar. Tharxion's eyes suddenly open and he sits up and looks around at the other's faces.

"Dad! You're alive," Yuskiocha weeps as he runs up to Tharxion. He rushes forward, hugging Tharxion, who cringes in pain as he tries to push back. Tharxion rises to a knee, his hand holding his side as Emerie and Amadeas take their place at his side.

"He's alive but he's not cured," Amadeas replies, lifting his armor to find a jagged piece of wood sticking out of his side. Amadeas pulls out a scroll, opening it toward the wound. The scroll begins to glow and suddenly the wound disappears as the wood splinters on the ground.

Tharxion rises back to his feet with his normal glow as the remaining scratches disappear. "What happened?"

"This guy attacked you," Crimpste replies as everyone turns to Thorarin.

"Did anyone attack him in return?" Tharxion replies as he looks at the other members

"Hey, we tried but Salordra got in the way," Mosenrath answers.

"Wow, your leader falls and nobody fights for his honor," Tharxion berates them.

"Don't be mad at us, we didn't realize it till it was too late," Mosenrath replies, taking a step forward.

"Plus, I was too distraught to attack anyway," Narlugo adds, trying to hide his tears from the other members.

"Oh my god, shut up just and go to sleep already," Salordra yells, silencing the guild.

"What do you think you're going to do about it?" Endaersal asks, pulling out his daggers.

"I will get you while you sleep," Salordra replies, turning his head away.

"Whatever, let's just go to sleep. We have a battle come daylight," Tharxion replies, turning to the chunks of wood at his feet. As the members separate, mumbling under their breath, Tharxion walks towards Thorarin standing by the fire.

"Hey, listen sorry about that whole thing," Thorarin says, his eyes glowing in front of the fire.

"All is forgiven," Tharxion replies. Tharxion pulls a scroll from his sleeve, watching as Thorarin walks out of the glowing light. His hand stops as the scroll dissipates, when suddenly Thorarin runs around the camp screaming while Tharxion looks on, laughing hysterically. As the effects wear off, Tharxion spots Amadeas and Emerie settling down over by the cliff.

"May I speak to you?" Tharxion asks as he walks toward them.

"Of course, what is on your mind?" Amadeas asks.

Tharxion takes a seat next to them as they place their weapons along the ground.

"I was just wondering why you guys didn't bring me back?" Tharxion asks, shutting his eyes as his head rests against one of the tent's poles. The two pause, before turning to Tharxion as he turns his head toward the night sky.

"We failed you," Emerie replies, letting out a deep breath.

"Oh, so what is that there?" Tharxion replies as he points to the stack of scrolls erupting from his bag.

"Yes, well then I guess we just wanted Molozel to have a shot," Emerie replies, shutting the bag.

"What if he would have failed?" Tharxion asks.

"Then we would have stepped in," Emerie and Amadeas reply in unison.

Tharxion nods his head, getting up when he spots an empty space for him feet away. Before he walks away, he turns back to see Thorarin, resting against the fence, still struggling to catch his breath. Tharxion smirks and settles down while looking around at the members that lay asleep around him. He gathers his thoughts, sitting down next to the fire with his legs crossed underneath him. He closes his eyes as he starts to float off the ground and the camp falls silent as the fire dwindles before him.

As darkness falls to the approaching sun, Tharxion opens his eyes to find that dawn is upon him and everyone making battle preparations. He looks around at everyone as his eyes catch sight of Salordra watching from his tent. Tharxion gets up and heads over to Salordra as his guards peel away, allowing him a straight shot inside.

"Was everything to your liking?" Salordra asks, turning his attention to Tharxion.

"I'd say so, seeing as we have survived the night," Tharxion replies, watching as Salordra kicks away a broken chair leg. Tharxion looks back and spots Yuskiocha loading up his satchel with ammunition.

"Hopefully your victory shall come swift and quick, for your sake," Salordra replies, looking over Tharxion's shoulder.

"You dare question my guild's strength?!" Tharxion roars. The entire guild stops, turning their attention to Tharxion, who keeps his eyes on Salordra.

"I do not, however anger can be a destroying force," Salordra replies.

"We will win, and it will be a battle that the Barazul will never forget," Tharxion replies, turning his attention to Anadae.

"Well then, I should tell you that we saw the Barazul leaders riding towards the ruins of Roa' Madi," Salordra replies as Tharxion turns his attention back to him.

"Was this out of interest or are you coming along?" Tharxion asks.

"Sorry to disappoint you, but my mind has not changed," Salordra replies.

Tharxion nods and then walks over to Narlugo to watch him pick up his final items.

"Hold on sorcerer, we might not be going, but we can still provide you with some information," Anadae yells, causing Tharxion to look back.

"Don't say it too loud! The Barazul may hear you!" Octegra yells from the top of a pile of crates.

As Narlugo looks on, Tharxion walks over to Anadae who leans over to whisper something into his ear. Tharxion jumps back in shock, looking over at Anadae who just shakes her head. Tharxion smirks in reply as he walks back to Narlugo and Lukain as they place their weapons back into position.

"All set," Narlugo says, turning to Lukain as he places a throwing dagger between his pant's leg and his boots.

"I see that, now what about the others?" Tharxion asks.

The three turn and look around as the other members surround them awaiting further command.

"Does that answer your question?" Lukain asks, watching as

each member pulls out a brownish crystal and throws it toward the ground. As the crystals shatter, horses appear from thin air underneath each member of the group

Tharxion nods he looks around at the group."Let us go for victory!" Tharxion yells, throwing his own crystal. Firmly on his horse, Tharxion takes off down the road as the others follow him. The members roar, taking off out of the camp, leaving nothing but a trail of dust.

With the members charging towards the remains of the Nomaz Crown, Narlugo makes his way to the front to Tharxion's side. "So, what did she whisper to you?"

"It's of no importance, just keep your focus forward," Tharxion replies as he charges along with Gunny and Nastale, leaving Narlugo behind.

As Narlugo tries to gather himself, Mosenrath pulls up to his side, trying to wipe the dust from his face. "Forget about it, let's win this for the BloodMinazue."

"I will," Narlugo whispers, turning to the road as stone buildings appear on the horizon. As the guild makes their way through the stone road, their eyes remain focused in front of them as the sun blazes above.

After a while, Crimpste suddenly turns to Tharxion and then to Gunny with eyes wide open. "Look ahead of us." Crimpste pulls a hand off the reins and points toward the mass of buildings.

Gunny and Tharxion look ahead, spotting four shadows on the side of the road.

"What are those things?" Baltor asks, squinting his eyes to get a better look.

"Bodies," Tharxion replies, rushing forward. Getting closer, the members slow as Tharxion dismounts from his horse at the foot of one of the green-skinned bodies. He walks up, wiping the sand from his eyes as he looks down at the bodies.

"Who are they?" Bulling asks as his horse stops among the others.

"They are members of the Minazue," Tharxion replies, inspecting the corpses and the horse skeletons by their side.

He turns toward the ruins and quickly turns around as he walks back towards his horse. With a sense of urgency, Tharxion charges, with the guild in tow, further covering the skeletons under a blanket of sand. As they approach the town in front of them, smoldering buildings hidden behind a crumbling stone wall cause a sense of despair to swallow up the members. Continuing to make their way into the city, their eyes struggle to take in the ashy ruins. Riding in, bodies lay around them. As they get to the ruins of one of the buildings, Tharxion and Necromyr drop off their horses, which turn back into brown crystals. Meanwhile, the rest remain with their eyes wide, inspecting the damage as the swirling winds kick up a mixture of bones and debris.

"Okay, Gunny I want you and Dockius to check the other side, while me and Necromyr check inside here," Tharxion says, making his way to the staircase in front of the broken doorway.

Dockius and Gunny roar, heading toward their area as Tharxion and Necromyr make their way up the stairs. As Tharxion and Necromyr walk inside the main room, the floor beneath them creaks, causing them to step back. After a brief pause, they continue inside, when Necromyr suddenly spots another body in the center of the room. The two of them rush over and find a piece of paper on its chest, an arrow impaling it in place. Necromyr kneels and removes the arrow as he hands the paper over to Tharxion. Tharxion looks down at the paper, and then begins to scratch his head as he looks at Necromyr.

"I can't read this," Tharxion says, taking a second look at the scribbled writing on the paper.

"Let me see if I can decipher it," Necromyr replies as he takes the paper from Tharxion. Necromyr stares at the paper and then quickly looks back at Tharxion when he shakes his head.

"Can you read it?" Tharxion asks, watching as Necromyr shakes his head.

"It's nothing I have ever seen," Necromyr replies.

"We need someone who is a wordsmith," Tharxion replies, looking around the room at the broken bookcases.

"Know anyone?" Necromyr asks.

"We need someone good with languages up here!" Tharxion yells out as everyone looks amongst themselves.

"I can try," Elash replies, dropping off his horse as his hood gets take caught by the swirling winds. Revealing a face scarred by wars and tattooed by tribal initiation, his orcish head turns toward Necromyr. As he arrives inside, Tharxion reaches back and hands him the paper, his eyes skimming over the writing. Elash then pauses, looking up at the two members as they give him some space.

"Can you read it?" Tharxion asks.

"It depends on what language it is," Elash replies as he lowers his head, each of his tattoos glowing a different color.

"Can you read it?" Necromyr asks, watching as the different glows fluctuate until they disappear, leaving only one.

"I certainly can," Elash replies.

"So, what does the paper say?" Tharxion asks.

"The Ruins of Roa' Madi shall be your resting place," Elash replies as suddenly the body turns to dust and blows away.

They follow the trail, watching as the other bodies do the same. Elash looks to Tharxion and Necromyr as they look back at him, grasping hold of their weapons. He walks over to them and hands the paper back to Tharxion, who snatches it from his grasp.

"Was that all it said?" Tharxion asks, looking down at the paper.

Elash nods his head as he watches the paper fall from Tharxion's hand onto the splinters of wood on the floor.

"Is there any word from Gunny and Dockius?" Necromyr asks, shifting their attention.

Elash and Tharxion turn to one another, shrugging as they turn outward in search of them.

***

Outside the ruins of another building, Gunny and Dockius walk past a stone sphere levitating above the ground as elemental energies flow around it. As they walk between the pillars splitting up the entrance, Gunny turns to Dockius, clutching his crossbow as he looks at the destruction. "Go inside and I'll look around for anything."

"Aye, Aye, Captain," Dockius replies, stepping inside the doorway out of Gunny's view.

Gunny smirks and turns toward the sphere as he starts to walk toward it. As Gunny gets to the sphere, he stands still and watches as the elements stop and spin toward the center of the stone. "Something isn't right."

Meanwhile, Dockius makes his way, using his staff as a walking aide as his crossbow sits on his back. Walking through, Dockius steps onto the balcony, where he looks over to find ghouls floating around the town's graveyard. He turns toward where Gunny is, when suddenly he hears a snicker come from inside the building. "Gunny, everything good over there?" Waiting for a response, Dockius's eyes look around the side of the building.

"Everything is quiet here...too quiet," Gunny replies, turning his attention away from the sphere. As Gunny steps onto the platform, suddenly the elemental energies turn to powder, and a lion's head appears out of Gunny's view.

Dockius aims his staff as he makes his way into the inn, when suddenly from out of thin air a bottle falls and crashes to the floor. Flexing his staff, Dockius looks on as a Barazul appears, drawing a giant sword. "Come and get it, warrior."

The warrior smirks and then looks past him, muttering something unbeknownst to Dockius. Before he can reach with his staff, Dockius stops and looks over his shoulder, his weapon frozen in his grasp. Dockius's eyes widen as suddenly two dwarves step out from the shadows, each carrying two daggers as they close in on him. As they slowly make their way, Dockius turns to the warrior in front of him. Before Dockius can catch a second glance of the warrior, it charges forward with its blade swinging the air.

Outside, the lion stalks Gunny as he walks around the broken cart on the rim of the platform. Suddenly, the lion pounces, sending Gunny crashing into the debris and through the shambles of the wall behind him. As his gauntlet catches the edge of the cliff, the lion steps forward, allowing Gunny to see its golden mane around its head.

"NO!" Gunny yells, grabbing the lion by the fur and sending it crashing into the ground below. Crying out a roar, the lion's chest gives way as its final breath escapes its body. Gunny turns to his slipping hand, grabbing hold with his free hand and pulling himself up.

Back inside, the crash rings through everyone's ear as the warrior is about to reach Dockius. Going in for the kill, the attacker approaches Dockius who breaks free, allowing him to block it with his staff. Dockius then spins around, tripping the warrior onto the floor as his sword slides a fingertip away. The two dwarves chuckle as they vanish into the shadows as Dockius looks for any sign of them. Dockius places his back against the wall as suddenly one of them reappears in mid-air, a dagger aiming at Dockius.

Just as it is about to strike, it's body stiffens as it drops to the floor, to Dockius's surprise. Dockius looks down and sees arrows within the dwarf's back, causing him to turn toward the doorway. To Dockius's surprise, Bulling stands in the doorway, reaching for another arrow from his quiver. Before Bulling can get another arrow into his bow, the warrior gets up and bashes Bulling, sending him crashing to the outside of the building. Dockius's eyes widen as the warrior suddenly turns back, smirking as blood drips from his mouth.

As Bulling falls to the floor, Viraxx dismounts from his horse, watching as Bulling rolls toward the edge of the platform. "Are you okay?"

As Viraxx looks down, Bulling lays motionless, suddenly releasing groan of agony as his eyes open a bit. Viraxx looks inside, watching as the warrior turns toward Dockius, blade in hand. Viraxx gets up, cracking the bones of his hands as he heads toward the doorway.

Inside, the warrior continues to creep toward Dockius as the other dwarf disappears behind him. As Dockius is about to take another step, it suddenly reappears, slicing the back of Dockius's legs with both blades.

The warrior's grin grows as he watches Dockius struggle to move his rubbery legs to break the numbness. The warrior steps up and stops directly in front of Dockius, grasping hold of his sword and raising into the air.

In his shadow, the dwarf chuckles, watching Dockius as his eyes follow the sword upward. The warrior turns his head toward it when suddenly a swirling portal appears, revealing a demonic hand which grabs hold of the dwarf's neck, snatching him toward the doorway. Turning his head, the warrior watches as the dwarf lands in front of the doorway where Viraxx waits for him. As the warrior watches, Dockius regains the feeling in his legs, retreating from the warrior. As Dockius loads a bolt into his crossbow, Viraxx rams his sword into the dwarf's chest, watching it stiffen in death. The enraged warrior turns to Dockius, seeing the front end of a bolt as it sits in the weapon. The warrior charges at Dockius, when it suddenly stops, looking downward as snowflakes rise from the ground. The warrior's eyes follow them as his skin freezes, rendering him unable to move.

Viraxx and Dockius begin to laugh as the warrior solidifies in ice. "Hey, Viraxx take care of his friend," Dockius says, pointing out the dead body in the doorway.

"Will do," Viraxx replies. Viraxx's eyes darken as the corpse sinks through the floor, a wailing zombie rising from the stones. Viraxx turns back to the warrior as the fiend rushes over to the warrior with arms flailing. As the warrior watches it approach, his ability to move returns and he breaks free from its frozen trap.

"Now it's my turn," Dockius says confidently as he fires a shot, striking the warrior in the center of his back. To the delight of the two, the warrior staggers back and forth, the zombie heading for him.

"Let's finish this guy off," Bulling says as he appears holding his bow in one hand and his side with the other.

The two nod and set their aim upon the dizzy warrior as he places his hand between the ridges of the pillar. Each then fires a shot, with Bulling striking him between the eyes and Dockius hitting him in the back of the head, causing the warrior to fall to his knees.

Viraxx is about to lay the final blow when the warrior's muscles give way, and he falls forward onto the floor. As the three expel a deep breath, Tharxion and the other members suddenly appear outside the doorway.

"Is everything okay in there?" Stelton asks, poking his head in the doorway.

"Check for yourself," Viraxx replies as he grabs the dead warrior and slides him down the ramp, landing at the feet of Stelton.

"Impressive, so where's Gunny?" Crimpste asks, watching as the members spit on the warrior's body.

"I thought he was over there," Dockius replies as he points over to the sphere's platform.

As the guild walks to the sphere, Endaersal spots Gunny's footprint over by the remains of the vendor cart. "Where did he go?"

"You don't think … " Lukain says, turning her head to the edge of the cliff. Turning, the group makes their way over, seeing the Barazul's body lying in the sand.

"Blucor, you and Apocol ride down to check if Gunny is under that," Tharxion says, looking over at the two men. Before either can reply, green fingers lift from out of the sand, revealing Gunny's location.

"A little help here?" a voice yells out. The members look over and find Gunny as his hand struggles to keep hold of the rocky edge.

"Forgarr and Bulling, mind lending us a hand?" Tharxion yells.

"I think we can do that," Forgarr replies as he and Bulling step towards the edge of the cliff.

The two reach out with their massive hands, grabbing hold of Gunny's wrist and arm. Trying to bring him onto solid ground, the two struggle as they try to pull Gunny out and balance themselves on the cliff. Slowly, they watch as Gunny gets more of his frame onto their level, allowing some more members to come forward to lend a hand.

As everyone steps back to give Gunny some space, Cappicola steps forward, extending a canteen toward him. "You know you could have just rode up the ramp right."

Gunny shakes his head as he pops open the top before pouring the water into his mouth. "If I had fallen to the floor then I would have."

"What happened?" Crusayder asks, watching as Gunny wipes the watery residue off his mouth.

"Well, I was looking around when suddenly a lion pounced, causing me to fall. Only I survived and it didn't," says Gunny. As he stumbles to his feet, Gunny looks around as the guild gets back on their horses.

"You coming?" Narlugo asks, picking up the leathery reins.

"Wouldn't miss it for a thing," Gunny replies, watching as his horse runs over from the sphere's platform to allow him to get on.

"Then I guess we're off again towards Roa' Madi," Tharxion says, striking the horse as he takes off down the town's exit. One by one, the members follow him out, leaving Gunny and Mernerva inside the town.

"No breaks for the weary I suppose," Mernerva replies with a smirk to Gunny.

"My poor armor," Gunny replies with a chuckle as he and Mernerva take off behind the members waiting at the bottom. As the two get to the bottom of the ramp, everyone heads down the sandy road towards Roa' Madi. Charging down the road, they look around as the peaks of mountains in the distance fade, revealing nothing beyond the vast deserts on both sides. Growing closer to the entrance of Roa' Madi, Dockius pulls up to the leaders in front, catching their attention as he slides between them.

"What is it, Dockius?" Tharxion asks.

"I feel something nearby," Dockius replies, looking down at the goosebumps along his wrist.

"Is it friend or foe?" Tharxion asks, searching around for anything.

"I'm unsure but I believe it to be one of us," Dockius replies, lowering his sleeve as he joins in on the search.

"Where is it?" Gunny asks, beginning his own search. Watching in front, a stone gate appears before them as it arches over the road.

Dockius looks over as sand falls from the top, suddenly spotting something laying beneath the archway. "There it is."

"Where do you see it?" Nastale asks, still searching.

"I see it," Mosenrath says as the guild continues toward the opening.

As the guild gets closer, each of the members spot the shadowy object amongst the cold stones along the road. Approaching the location, they find a rusty metal cage with a body inside, held shut by a lock jammed in the doorframe. They are surprised to find the blue body of a Minazue.

Thoranbuff dismounts and rushes over to the cage, grasping hold of the cage door as his eyes look for any sign of movement. "Can you hear me?" Failing to get a reply, Thoranbuff grabs hold of the lock to break it to no avail. As the lock screeches against the frame, the body lets out a groan as the entire guild steps forward.

"Gunny, break this lock for us," Nastale says, turning to Gunny.

Gunny walks up to the cage and inspects the lock before pulling his sword from off his back. "Step back Thoranbuff." Gunny lifts his sword and swings it down, striking the lock, causingThoranbuff to fall into the sand.

"Watch where you are swinging," Thoranbuff says, lifting himself back to his feet.

"I told you to step back," Gunny replies, placing his sword back on his back. As Thoranbuff mumbles behind him, Gunny grabs the lock and rips it off the frame, causing the door to creak open.

Tharxion steps toward the door and opens it wider, squeezing himself inside. As the members look on, Tharxion kneels next to the body as it begins to return to life.

"Is it alive?" Narrava asks, sticking her face up against the dangling chains along the cage.

"It seems so, but I can't heal her," Tharxion replies, looking down at the dried blood on the body's armor.

"Wow, well excuse me," Narrava replies.

"Methyl, can you and Amadeas come and move her outside?" Tharxion asks.

Methyl nods his head as he and Amadeas walk inside, dodging Tharxion as they grab the body's hands and feet. The two lift her up, making their way outside of the cage as the others circle around the body. As the rest of the guild looks on, Amadeas and Methyl begin to unroll their scrolls in search of a spell to return the body to health. After a few moments, her eyes open slowly as she looks around at the members.

"Greeting, my name is Tharxion, what is your name?" Tharxion asks, watching as the woamn continues to look around.

"My name is Krisania and I belong to the Troll clan," she replies, starting to sit up.

"How did you get inside that thing?" Thoranbuff replies, looking over at the cage.

"There is time for that, but for now we can help her up," Tharxion says, watching her get to a knee.

"It's okay, I had just landed in Nomaz Crown to collect some sand, when I was hit by something and now I am here," Krisania replies, feeling the back of her head.

Methyl walks over and begins to help Krisania to her feet when suddenly Krisania's eyes turn dark as an evil aura consumes her.

"Watch out Methyl!" Narrava screams.

Methyl turns his head, finding a demonic face staring back at him with pitch-black eyes and dark purple skin. Methyl's eyes widen as he retreats, watching as Krisania starts a chant in another tongue as she looks in his direction.

Narrava turns to Methyl and rushes to his side when suddenly Krisania screams, sending an unholy shockwave into them as they crash into the ground. Tharxion and the other members look on in shock as they grasp hold of their weapons as Krisania turns her evil sight onto them.

"We're not scared of you demon," Bulling replies, shaking as he places an arrow inside of his bow.

Krisania replies with a deep laugh as her twisted eyes darken.

As the members are about to charge, Krisania lets out a deafening roar, sending the entire guild fleeing in terror as she turns her attention back to Methyl and Narrava. "You shall not interfere with the Barazul."

Making her way over to their cowering bodies, she watches as they continue to struggle to gather themselves back to their feet. Krisania looks at Narrava, who collapses back down before looking over at Methyl as he slams his fists into the sand. She turns her attention back to Narrava as she kneels at her side.

"Don't you harm her," Methyl groans as he tries once more to get to his feet.

Krisania chuckles as she turns her attention back to Narrava. She grabs Narrava by her robe with one hand as her other hand raises a mace from behind her back. Krisania swings the mace, bludgeoning Narrava across the face, causing blood to spray from her mouth. Narrava screams in pain as Methyl looks on, trying to rise to his feet as she falls into the sand. Krisania turns to Methyl. "YOU'RE NEXT!"

Krisania creeps over to him with her mace dripping blood as it hangs by her side. As Krisania walks, the other members free themselves of the screaming and rush toward Krisania, realizing the predicament. Krisania stops and turns to see them running toward her with their weapons at the ready. She releases another ravaging scream, which knocks the members onto the floor, causing Methyl to fall back down. As the members try to get to their feet, Krisania walks over and grabs Methyl as a whirlpool appears from the sand. Krisania walks up to the edge and looks down at Methyl, suddenly tossing him in the swirling waves. She jumps inside as the others can only watch as the swirling ceases, returning the land to normal. As the members remain speechless, they suddenly spot Navarra's body lying on the sand.

Chapter Twelve

Torem and Forgarr rush over to Narrava, lifting her up before making their back to the others. As the two arrive, the members look on as Amadeas takes some parchment and places it against Narrava's bleeding mouth.

"Is she hurt badly?" Judication asks, watching as Amadeas tries to apply bandages to the wound.

"She'll be fine, it's only a flesh wound," Amadeas replies, sliding back as Narrava's eyes tear up.

"I don't think she wanted her anyway," Crimpste replies, rubbing his chin with his hand.

"What makes you think that?" Tabias asks.

"We now have one less guildie to fight with," Crimpste replies, silencing the rest of the guild.

"Enough, Gunny take them inside and find our enemy while Amadeas tries to heal her," Tharxion says, pointing toward an opening just beyond the archway.

"Certainly," Gunny replies with a bow before leading the members through the gate.

The members walk down into the dark tunnel, entering as Gunny watches on intently. Before Gunny can make his way through, Torem stops just shy of the opening and turns around in front of him.

"Yeah, that's right, I go first," Torem replies, flexing his arms.

"Yep, to death," Gunny replies, sending Torem stumbling down inside. Gunny then turns to Tharxion, before nodding his head as he enters the tunnel.

Tharxion turns to Amadeas just as he is about to finish reading the final words off his open scroll. Suddenly, Amadeas stops and looks down at Narrava as the blood dries and her eyes open.

"Are you okay?" Tharxion asks, watching as Narrava's eyes look all around.

"I think so," Narrava replies, pushing herself back to her feet with Tharxion and Amadeas's help.

"You took quite a blow back there, lucky for you I have spells for all wounds," Amadeas replies.

Tharxion turns to Amadeas and pulls out a yellow crystal from his bracers, handing it to Amadeas. "It's a Spirit Amber, so you can return to Salordra's camp in case of emergency."

Looking up in confusion, Amadeas looks at Tharxion as the crystal sits inside his palm. He then looks back at it, and places it inside his bag as he turns to Narrava. "Are you still ready to go?"

"Always ready for a taste of revenge," Narrava replies, brushing herself off.

Amadeas and Narrava gather their belongings as they walk over to the tunnel but stop before they can enter. Looking back, they find Tharxion still back beside the broken cage.

"Tharxion," Narrava yells, waving her hand back and forth.

"I'm coming, just making sure you guys don't get attacked by anything on the way in," Tharxion replies.

"Yeah, thanks," Amadeas says, turning to Navarra. They each take a deep breath, stepping into the darkness, leaving Tharxion outside.

Tharxion walks up to the tunnel, pausing for a second as his head turns in both directions before he finally walks inside. At the end of the tunnel he can see a light, allowing Tharxion to make his way back under the sun. Once back onto sandy ground, Tharxion finds himself among the crowd of members as they observe the area.

"So glad you could make it," Crusayder says, causing Tharxion to squint his eyes as he finds himself among the final row.

"I wouldn't let you have all the blood on your hands," Tharxion replies as he walks to where Stelton and Gunny are standing. As Tharxion gets to the front, Yuskiocha and Rose jump down from a stack of blocks along the pristine stone walls.

"See anything up there?" Stelton asks.

"We saw the Barazul army in the heart of this maze," Yuskiocha replies.

"Yes, and the four leaders are at the top of a pyramid," Rose adds.

"Great, then it shall be a battle that will go down in Minazue lore," Gunny says, lifting his sword into the air.

Tharxion nods his head, making his way to the front of the entire guild who fall silent just as he stops. "BloodMinazue, we have come upon an enemy that is unlike any we have seen in the past, and yet my belief in you is unmatched when it comes to our victory."

The guild roars and the walls shake as Tharxion looks at Yuskiocha and Narlugo, preparing their weapons. Tharxion then turns around and points down a corridor that leads out of the entrance as he makes his way with mace in hand. As the members follow behind, whistling sounds force their eyes toward the wall. The entire guild turns as they spot a Barazul sprinting on the top of the wall.

"Get him!" Gunny yells, watching as Dockius places his finger on the trigger of his crossbow. Tharxion suddenly steps in front of him, allowing the Barazul to get away.

"What'd you do that for? I had a clear shot!" Dockius asks, watching as Tharxion looks down the line of stones.

"Save your shots for the real battle, he's just a lamb," Tharxion replies, placing his mace back to his side.

Dockius lowers his crossbow, and watches as Tharxion walks back to the front of the line.

"Save your anger for the Barazul leaders," Torem replies as Dockius looks back. As the guild continues through the stone maze, they find the bodies of the guardians of Noa'madi, their human forms left bare of any trace of armor.

As the final row of members passes by, Narlugo walks beside Tharxion as the corridors continues to expand. "What do you think they're waiting for?" Narlugo whispers.

"No idea," Tharxion replies, watching as the stone walls turn toward the left. As the members go around the corner, arrows and bolts rain down from the sky, forcing everyone to dodge behind the various broken structures. As the arrows stop, they poke their heads out, suddenly spotting a group of hooded figures standing along the broken pillars beyond the wall.

"Master Crimpste, this is your time," Tharxion says.

Crimpste nods his head as he turns to Canosan and Shlippmack, who stand next to him awaiting orders. "Take those creatures out."

Canosan and Shlippmack smirk as they grab hold of their scrolls and locate the group of archers preparing another round. The two run out from behind the pillar and fire off pulses of energy from the folds of their scrolls. The archers scream as they jump out of the way at the last second before the missiles strike the wall. As explosions erupt, everyone steps out of hiding as they wait to see the next move. The two stop firing as their scrolls disintegrate, allowing the clearing smoke to reveal no trace of the archers.

"They're gone," Canosan says, turning back to the others.

"It would look like it, however we should still be cautious," Shlippmack replies, looking back at Canosan.

"Yeah, that's right Barazul! You better run from the mighty Molozel," Molozel says as he jumps out from behind the rock.

"What are you doing?" Saidin yells as another round of arrows rain down, causing the members to dive back behind their shields. However, this time the members look on in horror as arrows pierce the backs of Saidin and Molozel.

"NO!" Tharxion screams, watching as they collapse to the ground with the arrows piercing their back. Suddenly, in a fit of rage, Tharxion empties out his scroll bag and activates the magic within them. As the elemental energy erupts, one of the archers crashes into the hillside behind him while the rest sprint deeper into the maze. Tharxion turns back to the two fallen members and then rushes down the path, grasping hold of his mace. As Tharxion rushes away, the rest of the members rush to the two members, who cling to life.

"Amadeas, can you heal them?" asks Cappicola.

"I can try," Amadeas replies, turning a scroll toward Molozel. Just as he is about to use it, Molozel's bloody hand grabs hold of Amadeas's scroll, keeping the magic inside.

"Save your power and heal him, I wish to remember myself as a warrior," Molozel gurgles softly as his hand rolls off the parchment. Molozel's life fades as the guild turns its attention to Saidin, barely holding to life.

Amadeas kneels next to Saidin to inspect the arrow wounds throughout his back. "I need you to remove these, so I can get this to work." Visuvium and Baltor each grab hold of an arrow, removing them one by one from Saidin's back as Saidin moans in agony.

"Done," Visuvium and Baltor say in unison.

Amadeas looks back at Saidin as he unrolls a scroll, placing it against the bloody wounds, which it starts to heal. As the last puncture wound disappears, Saidin's eyes reopen. "You still with us?"

Saidin gathers his wits about him as he rolls over to his side. "Is everything okay?"

"Well, Molozel is dead and Tharxion, out of rage, is chasing the archers," Narrava replies.

Saidin frowns as his eyes fall upon Molozel's corpse, lying on the ground next to him. "Why didn't you use it on him?"

"He told us to let him go and heal you," Amadeas replies, watching as Saidin tries to get up.

As Saidin gathers to his feet, he wipes the tears from his eyes and turns toward the open corridor. "They shall pay for what they've done!" Saidin and the members run down the path, but stop suddenly when they realize Thoranbuff and Mosenrath are still beside Molozel's corpse.

"You guys coming?" Tabias asks.

Mosenrath looks over to Tabias before turning his attention back to the body at his feet. "We shall when his body fades into the sand."

The members nod their heads before turning their attention back to the path as they continue to run after Tharxion. After a while, the running members spot a rock, where Tharxion sits with his mace in his lap. As the members begin to approach him, Tharxion looks over and then turns his attention back toward the opening next to him.

"What's the matter?" Lukain asks Tharxion, who turns back.

Before Tharxion can reply, his eyes widen as he spots Saidin standing at Amadeas's side. "Saidin, is that you?"

"Yes, brother it is me," Saidin replies, watching as Tharxion jumps down from the rock.

Tharxion smiles and then turns to Amadeas who looks back with uncertainty. "Where is Molozel?"

The guild falls silent as Amadeas takes in a deep breath, wiping some of the sweat from his forehead. "He is gone, I was trying to heal him, but he wanted me to save Saidin," Amadeas replies.

"We shall take the Barazul down, not only in honor of the Minazue but in honor of our fallen brothers like Methyl and Molozel," Tharxion replies.

"So, what are you waiting here for?" asks Saidin.

"For you guys," Tharxion replies, pointing out into the opening. The members walk over and spot the Barazul army as they peek from the corridor.

"So, are we going to let them wait?" Gunny asks.

"It wouldn't be right," Tharxion replies as he lifts up his mace.

"Well then, let's go," Nastale says, lifting his staff.

The guild gathers up and walks out of the corridor into a vast area, where a large pyramid in the center is surrounded by pillars. As the guild walks toward the pyramid, they see that the entire Barazul army stands at all levels, with some at the very bottom and the leaders at the very top. Continuing their approach, the members pull out their weapons as they stare at the Barazul army. Stopping in their tracks, they look up to see the four leaders plus Krisania standing at the very top, looking back at them.

"I guess we'll make the first move," Tharxion says, turning to Nastale.

"Let's change things up!" Nastale yells.

Suddenly Oxala whistles as the guild watches leafs sprout from his limbs and his skin turns brown. Sizlack, on the other hand, roars as his arms fall away and wings take their place. Nastale smiles, turning back to Tharxion and Stelton, checking to see if they are all prepared.

"See, Octegra isn't the only one who has one," Tharxion says as he points to the Mana Breaker at his side.

Tharxion then turns to the four leaders, and smirks before letting out a roar as the members do the same. Just as the members are about to attack, some of the Barazul members morph into bears of different shades, along with big cats of different patterns. Suddenly, the air begins to swirl with the scent of battle as the two groups stand still, waiting for the other to make a move. Finally, the silence is broken when both sides begin their charge as the Barazul leaders watch from the top.

"It will be better if you fight your equal," Tharxion replies as the Mana Breaker crashes into its Barazul counterpart.

As the fight rages on, Gunny swipes at a Barazul, stunning it, just as he realizes that Forgarr is down a level with three Barazuls surrounding him. Gunny pushes his enemy off the pyramid onto the floor and then jumps onto one of Forgarr's enemies, sending his sword through its chest. As Gunny gets up, another jumps onto his back, aiming his sword downward until a sudden fireball comes and blows it away. Gunny looks back and sees Apocol blowing smoke from his scroll before collapsing to the floor. He turns to see a robed Barazul continuing to fire prismatic blasts toward Apocol.

Meanwhile on the other side, Stelton watches as three bears charge him as he shoots an arrow which splits, striking two between the eyes. Another arrow bounces off the bear's skin when it jumps on top of Stelton, trying to maul him until Cappicola bashes it off. Cappicola looks down, pulling Stelton up as he turns back and charges back into the heart of the battle.

As the mage continues to hit Apocol, Crimpste sneaks up behind it until he stands behind it with his hands out wide. Crimpste grasps hold of its hands, causing it to drop the scroll on top of Apocol. Crimpste shoves it and unrolls a fire scroll from his sleeve, releasing a wave of flames. As it falls to the floor, Apocol smirks until suddenly a javelin pierces through his chest, causing him to collapse to the floor.

Crimpste watches as Apocol's eyes shut as the Barazul pulls out his bloody javelin before turning it toward him. The Barazul runs toward Crimpste as he throws the javelin, barely missing Crimpste. The Barazul looks at the javelin and then reaches back to pull out an axe. However, just as the Barazul is about to reach it, Crimpste pulls out a second scroll and throws it at the Barazul, blinding him in an explosion of light. Crimpste reaches back for his wand when suddenly it regains its senses and continues its attack. Just as the Barazul is about to strike again, a meteoric rock falls from the sky and sends the warrior crashing through the floor, leaving its body in a cindering hole. Crimpste turns back and sees two familiar faces standing in the entrance of the valley.

"Nice of you to join the fight finally," Crimpste says, striking another enemy in the back with his wand.

"We couldn't let you have all the fun," Mosenrath replies as he and Thoranbuff rush toward the battleground. Suddenly, from out of the shadows, the three archers appear, and rush in from behind, aiming their swords toward the bottom of the pyramid.

At the bottom, Amadeas struggles to get the upper hand against a Barazul, while throwing scrolls to keep his allies alive. Mosenrath looks over to Amadeas, and then turns to the archers as he rushes over, lifting his hands up as a greenish glow covers his hands. Suddenly, a mountainous tree crashes through the wall, sending chunks of stone everywhere. It charges in the direction of the archers as they prepare to step up onto the stairway. Just as they are about to get to Amadeas, the archers stop in their tracks, feeling the quaking earth beneath their feet. Turning around, the archers get consumed by its massive shadow as they retreat. Their eyes wide, the archers attempt to load their bows as the tree topples over and lands with a thud. Sending up sand in all direction, the tree melts down, leaving behind only an indentation where the archer's broken bodies remain.

Amadeas turns to Mosenrath, waving his wand as it creates a magical shield in front of Tabias just as a strike is about to land.

"Need some help?" Mozenrath ask, watching Amadeas as he uses his mace to block a sword. The feather along Mozenrath's skin drop off, giving way to leaves as his feet turn to roots. Mosenrath raises his wooden arms up as the floor beneath the members releases green pods and a greenish mist that covers all the wounded members. As the pods shrink, Mosenrath turns around in shock as a Barazul stands next to him, with a scroll facing his direction.

"Don't just stand there move those roots!" Yuskiocha screams, stabbing a Barazul and tossing another one to the floor below.

Mosenrath turns away and runs as he lifts a chunk of soil with each step. As Mosenrath is running away, the Barazul smirks as fireballs shoot out from the scroll, honing in on Mosenrath. In a last resort, Mosenrath falls forward, allowing the fireballs to crash into the ruins. Mosenrath gets up and brushes off his leaves until his wooden fingers reach for the leaves on his head. He then brings his arm downward, feeling nothing as he finds only ash. As the ashes fall from his hand, Mosenrath looks up and sees the Barazul laughing hysterically.

"Sorry, Amadeas," Mosenrath says as feathers erupt from his scaly skin. As the Barazul looks on, Mosenrath puts his hands in front of him when suddenly a scroll manifests, releasing a blast and sending it high into the air. It crashes on two Barazuls, who are just about to fire off shots at an unsuspecting Tyrodris.

Tyrodris swings his blade, slicing the minion in half and then swings again as the controller blocks it with his sword. Tyrodris swings again, but it is blocked again and this time the minion answers with a kick to Tyrodris's stomach, which sends him back first into a boulder. Tyrodris shakes off the blow and then charges toward the Barazul, tackling it to the floor. As Tyrodris is about to gain the upper hand, suddenly roots appear from the ground and entangle his legs, leaving him prone.

The Barazul gets up and raises his sword to strike Tyrodris, but before he can a demonic fiend appears and takes the strike. Tyrodris manages to break free and looks over to find Tharxion using his foot to pry his mace from a Barazul's chest. "Thanks for that."

"Just remember you owe me one," Tharxion roars as he smashes down another Barazul.

On the level above, Nosferatmoo watches as Bulling fends off three Barazuls as he fires off two bolts, pinning the Barazul to the wall. As Bulling is about to fire off another shot, Nosferatmoo jumps down and slices the Barazul's throat. After a wave of blood splashes onto the stones, Nosferatmoo turns to Bulling, who shakes his head in disapproval. Suddenly a Barazul swings a sword at Bulling, who barely manages to dodge it.

Nosferatmoo reaches out, creating a rift of bubbling energy which sends the Barazul towards him. With the Barazul charging him, Nosferatmoo rams his sword into its chest and then smashes the skull with his mace, sending the Barazul collapsing to the floor. "Two shots before he hit the floor." Nosferatmoo then puts his sword back in its sheath as he looks over to Bulling.

"One second," Bulling says, suddenly turning and firing a bolt, striking a charging Barazul in the chest.

The Barazul attempts to remove the bolt with its last breath, but

151

just drops to the floor with its sword still in hand. Bulling then turns back to Nosferatmoo as he places his crossbow on his back. Before either can say anything, Tharxion charges through the middle of them, watching as he runs toward the top. Bulling and Nosferatmoo look back down and see the class leaders charging behind Tharxion as the rest are continuing the fight below.

As Tharxion gets to the top, the main Barazul leader, King Ronos, points at Krisania, and then looks back to Tharxion. Krisania turns to Tharxion as she raises her mace to the darkening sky before letting out a deafening screech. She runs at Tharxion who begins to brace himself for the blow when suddenly Gunny appears and pushes Tharxion out of the way. Krisania collides with Gunny who backs up a bit, but looks up as Krisania struggles to hold her ground.

Gunny takes his shield and bashes Krisania down onto the walkway, causing her to nearly slide off the edge. As Krisania tries to get up, she looks and sees Gunny walking toward her with his sword to his side. She rises and takes out her wand, but as she tries to hit Gunny he blocks it, sending it off the pyramid. Krisania watches as the wand snaps in half as it hits the floor and Gunny continues to approach. She grasps hold of her mace and tries to swing, only to watch Gunny's massive hand grab hold of her hand, stopping it cold. As Krisania struggles to get free, Gunny raises his sword and knocks her unconscious. The other class leaders watch as Gunny takes Krisania by the neck and walks her over to the edge, hanging her body in the air.

"You dare not save your creation?" Tharxion yells.

King Ronos turns to Gunny and then turns to Tharxion, completely ignoring what he had said.

"Gunny, drop his pet to the floor with the rest of the worms," Tabias says as everyone's attention turns to Gunny.

Gunny smirks as he turns to the unconscious Krisania, and looks down at the floor of the fallen Barazul bodies. Gunny releases his hold and Krisania falls to the floor with a massive thud. Gunny shakes his head before walking over to Tharxion and the other class leaders.

"Hey wait, where is Amadeas?" Tharxion asks.

"I'm down here," a voice replies. The class leaders look down to see Amadeas running through the fighting, trying to reach the top. As Amadeas is making his way, he stops in his tracks when a Barazul warrior suddenly steps in front of him. Amadeas raises a spellbook up, which releases a dome of light over him just as the warrior lifts his axe. As the axe is in motion, it suddenly drops to the ground, to the delight of Amadeas and the other leaders. The warrior suddenly falls on top of it, enabling Amadeas to see Cappicola and Yuskiocha with their bows in their hands. Cappicola and Yuskiocha kick the body out of the way, allowing Amadeas to continue up the stairs.

"Nice of you to join us," Crimpste says as he takes out a scroll and his mace.

"You'd be late too if you had to heal an army," Amadeas replies as the leaders gather up in front of the Barazul leaders. The four look at each other, and then gather their weapons in preparation for battle.

Tharxion turns to Nastale who nods as his face and body grow snow white hair, which covers his bear-like features.

As the leaders wait in silence despite the chaos of the battles below, Gunny raises his sword and charges at the enemy leaders with Nastale in toe. Narlugo releases a lightning bolt from a scroll, aiming it toward Elementia Vorrais who battles it off with a spell of her own. Nearby, Gunny charges into King Ronos and Nastale runs toward Jadin, who grasps hold of his icy horns. As the three leaders begin their battles, Golos Hinnerog takes a gulp of his ale, which Cheshete smacks out of his hand. Golos Hinnerog then looks up and meets the end of Cheshete's dagger, pointing directly into his face.

Golos Hinnerog gulps and takes a step back before pulling his daggers from out of his armor and swings at Cheshete. Cheshete blocks the attack and attempts to deliver one of his own, but Golos Hinnerog blocks it with his other dagger. With both their weapons pushing against each other, Golos Hinnerog kicks Cheshete, sending him sliding past the other leaders. As Cheshete tries to shake it off, Golos Hinnerog twirls a throwing dagger and slings it at Cheshete, who dodges the dagger as it rips a hole in his cloak. Cheshete glances back at the other leaders before looking back at Golos Hinnerog, seeing him laughing at him. Cheshete gets up and runs past Narlugo, just as he pulls out an elemental seed from inside his hand and slams it into the ground, releasing its magic into him. Suddenly, Narlugo's body tightens as chains of elemental energy flows through his veins, connecting to Elementia Vorrais's staff.

Elementia Vorrais looks down with glowing eyes as she fires off a spell from a hidden scroll, sending it at Narlugo, who dodges it. Narlugo charges as his arms turn into a mixture of rock and crystal that strike her down onto the floor. As Elementia Vorrais gets up, Gunny and King Ronos swing their swords at each other. The two begin to try to push the other off as Cheshete sprints towards Golos Hinnerog with his daggers at his side. Golos Hinnerog spots him and takes aim as Cheshete charges forward. As Cheshete runs, he dodges the strike and jams his dagger into the back of his leg. Golos Hinnerog angrily rips out the dagger from his leg and looks over at Cheshete as he throws the dagger on the floor.

Cheshete smirks as Golos Hinnerog suddenly looks down, feeling the muscles in his leg spasm. "Got to love Poison."

Golos Hinnerog looks up in spite as he falls to his knees, unable to get up. He watches as Cheshete pops the cork out of a poison vial and dips his dagger in the green ooze inside. Cheshete drops the vial and just as it hits the floor, he suddenly vanishes from Golos's sight.

Golos looks all over when suddenly a sharp pain rushes through his body. He grimaces as he turns his head, finding Cheshete behind him with his dagger in his back. Golos turns back as he falls limply to the ground, just as Cheshete rips his dagger out of his back.

Cheshete looks up and finds Gunny still trying to break through King Ronos's defense. As Gunny continues his push, suddenly a demonic spear of lightning appears and strikes King Ronos, weakening him momentarily. King Ronos looks on, barely holding his sword as Gunny begins to roar before charging him.

As Gunny charges, he swings his sword just as King Ronos puts up his own to try to block the strike. As the swords strike each other, King Ronos's sword shatters as Gunny's sword slices into King Ronos's chest, causing him to twist to the floor. Gunny looks down, preparing to deliver the final blow, when suddenly a lightning bolt crashes through the middle of the platform. The blast sends him onto his back as King Ronos remains still on the stone floor.

Elementia turns away from Gunny toward Narlugo, who struggles to get up, as she drops her staff, pulling out a sword from underneath her cloak. As she walks over, she stops when suddenly a spear falls to the floor and releases four wolves, each made of a different elemental energy. Just as Narlugo gets up, the wolves release a chilling howl as they tackle Elementia to the floor. Narlugo watches as Elementia tries to fight them off, and Gunny recovers to his feet, watching as King Ronos stands with a hand over his ribs. Gunny grabs his sword off the ground and jumps at King Ronos, sending him back to the ground. Gunny pins him down as he takes his sword in both hands and thrusts it into King Ronos's chest. Gunny exhales and rolls off King Ronos, leaving his sword in the corpse of the Barazul king. As Gunny gathers his breath, the wolves dissipate into particles, leaving Elementia cowering, to Narlugo's delight.

Narlugo looks at Elementia and shakes his head as he extends his hand. His hand suddenly creates a magic scroll, which suddenly releases an orb of thunder, striking Elementia, causing her to spasm, and then fall limp.

As the guild leaders gather up, Nastale continues the search for Jadin on the level below. As Nastale walks down the walkway, Jadin squats down behind a boulder to try to keep out of his sight. Just as Nastale approaches the boulder, Jadin pops out and sends him off the walkway, which he barely holds onto with a paw.

Jadin walks over, chuckling as Nastale struggles to hold on, trying to use his claws to pull himself up. Jadin kneels and places his staff under Nastale's claws, prying them out of the gravel between the stones. Just as Jadin begins, a bright light appears from above, which releases a wave of light that strikes and stuns Jadin. As Jadin spins dizzily, he finds Tabias behind him, holding out his sword.

Tabias smirks and then rams his sword into Jadin's chest, causing him to drop his staff onto the ground. For a moment, Jadin grasps hold of the sword at his side, but then his hand slides off as Tabias twists and rips out his own sword. As Jadin falls to the floor, Tabias quickly drops his sword and kneels next to Nastale, grabbing hold of his hand. Tabias pulls him up and helps him back to his feet as the other leaders look from the floor above.

As the leaders gather up to the top, they let out a massive roar that the members below echo. After the final Barazul is down, all the members climb to the top along with the guild leaders.

"Have we won?" Grugnor asks, looking around at the fallen leaders.

"It appears so," Tharxion replies, watching as Gunny walks over to the corpse of King Ronos.

Gunny kneels and slices off his head before placing it in a bag on his back. "It's a gift for Kolozi."

"Sure it is, now members! Let's return to Dapalos and celebrate this victory," Tharxion replies.

One by one, the members throw down their crystals as their horses take shape along the platform. They jump onto their steeds and quickly dash off into the open sands outside. When the final hoofprint is silenced, the sudden swirling of four purplish rifts forming on top of the leaders breaks the silence. One by one, the leaders jump out and appear, looking around at the remains of the battle.

"Those fools think they've won," King Ronos chuckles, looking around at the other leaders.

"They did win," Jadin says as he jumps up to the top with the rest of the leaders.

"Certainly not, this was just a battle for the war ahead," King Ronos replies.

"So what did we fight them for?" Elementia Vorrais asks as she brushes off her robe.

"Did none of you listen to the plan? Our sorcerer was going to create shadow portals so we could not lose this fight, even if we were to die," King Ronos replies. The three other leaders look at each other, and then turn back to him nodding their heads in agreement.

"Well then, let us head back to Athial, I feel a disturbance which requires our attention," Jadin says as he conjures up a whirlpool in the stones.

"Which is?" Golos Hinnerog asks, looking down at the swirling stones.

"The Ring of Sight has shown itself in the Drago Plains," Elementia Vorrais says, watching as the other leader's eyes widen in shock as Jadin completes the whirlpool.

"Off to Athial we shall go," King Ronos says as he jumps in, holding onto his crown.

Elementia Vorrais then walks up and jumps in, Golos Hinnerog jumping after her. Jadin walks up to the swirling pool and takes a brief look around and jumps through, just before it returns to normal.

***

Back in Dapalos, Kolozi and the other Minazue elders await in the throne room when a guard comes running inside.

"Sire, the BloodMinazue have returned victorious!" the guard says as they get out of their chairs.

Scurrying out of the castle, they find the guild awaiting them on their horses. The members get off and follow the elders back into the throne room. As the members look around, the elders begin to sit back down as massive smiles creep onto their faces.

"Congratulations, BloodMinazue for your victory in Roa' Madi!" Kolozi roars.

The members roar as Gunny leaves the group with the bag in hand to bring it over to Kolozi. Kolozi looks down at the bag and opens it wide, suddenly dropping the bag in surprise.

"What's the matter?" Gunny asks, reaching for the open bag.

"This bag is empty," Kolozi replies, kicking the bag closer to Gunny. The entire guild gasps in shock, when suddenly Legorn rushes inside the throne room from the outside.

"Sire, I have important news about the Barazul!" Legorn says, huffing and puffing out of breath.

"Like what, that the Minazue is doomed?" Kolozi asks.

"No, on the contrary, the guild defeated the leaders, but the leaders replicated before returning to Athial after the members left," Legorn replies as Kolozi looks over at the guild.

"My apologies BloodMinazue. For your achievement, I now give enough gold as a thank you from all of us," Kolozi replies, looking back at a table of large brown sacks.

"That is greatly appreciated," Tharxion says, watching as the rest of the guild stares at the table and the couple of coins laying around.

"Come outside, we must announce your victory to the entire city," Kolozi says, motioning his hand out the door.

As the four elders and the guild walk outside, roaring cheers await them as commoners flood the grounds.

"Here are your heroes, the mighty BloodMinazue!" the four elders yell, renewing the roaring of the crowd. As the crowd continues to cheer and stomp, Tharxion makes his way forward to Kolozi's side.

"Where is this Athial?" Tharxion asks.

"At the other end of the world, outside of our kingdom," Kolozi whispers.

"That is good to hear," Tharxion replies as he heads back over to the other members who are continuing to cheer.

"We are the mighty Minazue, and we fear no being!" Kolozi yells. The members look at one another, and then turn back, letting out a massive roar that echoes throughout the city.

Epilogue

"That is the end," Groza says, looking around at the compatri-
ots that surround him. He smiles to see that even the Symbol-
isk-hating bartender had sat himself on the other side of the counter.
Before anyone can speak a word, the door to the tavern swings open,
allowing a tall, shadowy figure to enter the room. As it places its
monstrous hand upon the caving doorway, it steps inside as everyone cautiously stares in silence.

"I am looking for the keeper of the BloodMinazue's tale," the
figure bellows out, causing the occupants of the bar to separate. As
Prozper and Groza remain in the figure's view, Groza turns back and
closes the book before bringing it forth.

"That would be I," Groza answers.

The figure grins, revealing a mouth of yellowish sharp teeth the
skin on his hands suddenly peeling back. They watch as ice begins to
surge up from his arm through his fingertips, sending a chill through
the room.

"I can't move," Prozper screams, causing Groza to look over to
see a chain of ice wrapping around the barstool and creeping up his
body. The chain continues forward, turning every inch of Prozper
into solid ice until it finally wraps around his neck. Chilling his body
to the core, the ice glistens underneath the glow of the torches. As
his movement ceases, Groza slowly turns back to find the figure still
standing in the doorway with the skin back around his hand.

"What did you do?" Groza yells, bringing the book closer to his chest.

"He was wanted for leaving an entire tribe of elves frostbitten," the figure replies, turning back outside. Before anyone can reply, the figure disappears as the silence inside the room gives away to a bundle of whispers.

Groza looks over at Prozper, still frozen in place, when suddenly he falls onto the floor, shattering into chunks. As the ice begins to melt down into the cracks of the floor, Groza looks back as the bartender wipes off the residue left behind on the counter.

"You pushed him," Groza says, turning around in his chair.

"Sorry, but he was taking up precious space," the bartender replies, reaching underneath the lip of the counter. Before Groza can speak, the bartender pulls out a glass with a brown liquid inside and slides it over to him.

"What is this for?" Groza asks as his hand wraps around the glass.

"For closing the final chapter and for keeping this place full of patrons," the bartender replies.

Groza faintly smirks before bringing the glass to his mouth and drinking down the contents in a single gulp. Once the final drop was gone, Groza places it back down as the chatter around them returns to a normal pitch.

Reviews are crucial to indie authors like me. If you enjoyed this book, please leave me a review! It helps me and it helps others find my book, too! Thank you!

Also, check out my other books:

The Adventures of George and Reggie

The Adventures of George and Reggie 2: KING ORCAN'S REVENGE

Murdio